DIARY OF A TREE SITTER

DIARY OF A TREE SITTER

❀

A Monologue

By

R. R. ROPER

iUniverse, Inc.

New York Lincoln Shanghai

Diary Of A Tree Sitter
A Monologue

iUniverse, Inc.

For information address:
iUniverse, Inc.
2021 Pine Lake Road, Suite 100
Lincoln, NE 68512
www.iuniverse.com

ISBN: 0-595-29350-6

Printed in the United States of America

Contents

❀

Day 1.

"One impulse from a vernal wood
May teach you more of man,
Of moral evil and of good,
Than all the sages can."

—Wordsworth

❦   ❦   ❦

Well, here I am, perched on a platform a hundred and fifty feet in the air, on the side of a beautiful redwood tree, in the middle of a forest of redwood trees, protesting against a corporation dedicated to their destruction.

To be fair I should say that the corporation whose practices I am protesting gave me permission to build this platform, and to hang out here as long as I am able. I suspect they think that a protest of this nature is preferable to a massive demonstration of fifty or so Greenpeace zealots carrying placards and marching noisily down the main street of Eureka, California or heaven forbid, San Francisco. I might get some press initially but nothing of any significance.

My platform is rather elaborate since I intend to spend 100 days up here, ostensibly protesting the wanton destruction of the forests all over this blessed country. Ostensibly, I say, because I have my own agenda, which is to escape the constant and irrepressible chaos in my life caused by the modern insistence on spoken communication between spouse, children, friends, associates, solicitors, doctors, family, et cetera. And, to accomplish this communication through every device thus far invented by man, including telephones, cell phones, beepers, walkie-talkies, fax machines, e-mail, voice mail, real mail, radio, the all-surround sound TV, and you name it.

God, it's hard to get away.

Therefore, I devised a plan to maybe contribute to a worthy cause while satisfying this absolute obsession of mine to get rid of all of these interruptions, and somehow sequester myself for a period of time, to think, and write, and just be. It took me some time to find a way to do this and I must say that I would not be able to be where I am if it were not for my wife and daughter and a host of friends who believe my sole purpose in being up here is to draw attention to their cause for preserving the natural environment. A cause, which I must say, is at the expense of thousands of people who make their living in the lumber industry. People, who, I believe, are trying to sustain the forests while still preserving their rights as capitalists under the provisions and guarantees of the constitution.

Be that as it may, as I said, my platform, although not a suite at the Waldorf, is as luxurious and comfortable as a platform a hundred and fifty feet off the ground can be. The platform itself is made of wood (I wonder where that came from if not from a forest), with good supports beneath and to the side of it, and with a roof, also made of wood. The whole thing is covered with a stout tarpaulin that can be pulled down around the sides so that the interior can remain dry and somewhat draft free.

My son-in-law, who is a skilled carpenter, agreed to build the platform for me. He and several of his friends designed and built it almost overnight. In order to get him and the materials up to the height I desired he had to rig a fairly sophisticated pulley system with a large metal basket suspended from a steel cable. I now use the system for the supply of my provisions and to lower my waste bucket.

I do not have a chair. I shall have to content myself with sitting on a cushion on the floor to eat, and read, and most important, write. I have a laptop computer on which to record my stories, my thoughts, and day-to-day activities. It is the only concession I have made to modern technology, otherwise I am completely dependent on the good attentions of my support staff for food, water, charged batteries for my laptop, waste removal, and whatever else I must have in order to survive here on my perch, up in the heavens with the birds, the whispers of the wind, and the wanderings of my own mind.

It is a glorious adventure, simply glorious, given the fact that I am 70 years old and probably should know better. But then in one's declining years the heart yearns for action, and excitement, and drama, and something to do other than simply getting ready to die.

I speak lovingly of my support group but I must say that my wife, who is 13 years younger than me, did not really take to the idea of my leaving her for three months to go sit in a tree. She is very conventional; she has a problem that way. It's a flaw in her character.

When I first broached the idea she said, "Are you crazy?" and I recalled hearing the wife of the new owner of the Buffalo Bills football team ask the same question regarding his purchase of the Bills. She said exactly the same thing as my wife, "Are you crazy?" to which he replied, "No, I'm 70." I answered my wife with the same statement. She threatened to throw a tantrum but I beat her to it, saying "I'm going and that's all there is to it, damn the torpedoes and full speed ahead." I think my reference to torpedoes in connection with my intent to perch in the trees threw her mind into such confusion that all she could muster was, "and I hope one of those torpedoes flies up your butt!"

Eventually, she grudgingly accepted the idea although not with any great enthusiasm. The next thing I knew she was planning my whole expedition. You would have thought I was going to Everest. I had to remonstrate vigorously to discourage her from ordering room service for me while I was in my high hideaway.

The fact that I am 70 years old contributes a little more attention to my attempt to get away than I would like. Somehow the story got out, and of course, our omniscient media exposed me in all my glory to the world. Suddenly I find myself a minor celebrity whose boring exploits will be followed relentlessly day-by-day in the press, and TV, in radio news reports, and probably the National Examiner (replete with sordid details of my intercourse with birds). That is, until I finally outlast them, cease to be news, and they all forget I ever existed, as they race each other to the next unusual or horrific event the world continually provides. I will welcome that day. In the meantime I will do my absolute best to completely ignore them.

My son-in-law built me a small, crude desk that stands about a foot off the floor much like a Japanese dining table, so that I can sit upright while typing at my laptop. It will also serve as *my* dining table.

I have several ideas for writing, essays mainly, although I may compose a short story or two. It all depends on my mood. Right now I shall content myself with becoming adjusted to my new environment.

It is beautiful up here. I cannot see much except trees, and a small portion of the horizon that is usually cloudy but lovely nonetheless. It is beginning to rain, I can expect a lot of that up here, but I do not mind. It will only serve to make my hundred days somewhat damper than my library at home. I won't let it bother me.

I will try to write in my diary everyday, but I want to get to my other writing, so I will only record some of my thoughts in my journal. I don't expect anything of any significance to happen up here while I'm in limbo, incommunicado, and incognizant of the world down below.

Day 2.

"The woods are lovely, dark and deep…"

—Robert Frost

❧   ❧   ❧

Damn, this is wonderful. I have been writing from sun-up to dark. I didn't even take many breaks except to eat something. The creative juices are flowing at an unbelievable rate. And, the great part of it is I can write purely; without hesitation; thinking that I have to stay within bounds; that I can't use certain words; must be politically correct; must stay with the traditional formulas of what constitutes a novel, a short story, an essay, whatever. I don't have to observe any of that foolishness. I can write whatever I damn well please. I can write uninterrupted, and say whatever I want without criticism of any kind; write in my own style; my own way; I can use language as I wish, and to hell with the critics, the public, the publishers, and God himself. I will write what I want to write and that is that.

Not that I'm so proud of what I write. It's just that I like to think of myself as an author. I don't know, it just sounds prestigious. I would like to write something poignant and pithy but then poignant and pithy are really not in style these days. Therefore, I'll settle for titillating and thoughtful. If I can't achieve that then I will throw down my laptop, and stomp disgustedly from the room. Oops. Can't do that now can I?

I forgot to say anything about writing poetry. I think it's an unforgivable sin, unless you're a Robert Frost or a T. S. Eliot, but I'm guilty of it, and since no one will ever read this mindless chronicle I'll go ahead and sin to my heart's content. I'll start with this one:

It helps to get it out of me,
To spill these words
Across a page;
To let my mind and soul
Indulge in intercourse,
To some sweet music,
That moves majestically
Through spirit only;
To speak the poet's tongue,
(Though poorly)
To relieve some inner pressure;
To escape from mundane care;
To feel the spirit's freedom,
And note it here.

Day 3.

"...I stand not high it may be,
but, alone."

—Rostand

✤   ✤   ✤

It has rained almost constantly since I made the ascent to my platform, which means that I live in a cocoon made of a heavy tarpaulin. It is close and damp. The feeble glow from my oil lamp yields a warm but less than sufficient light to the interior. It also puts a smoky fragrance into the air that is somewhat unpleasant and keeps me in fear of a fire. Occasionally, the fumes become somewhat dense and obnoxious when the wind blows hard, and instead of drawing the fumes out, simply pushes them inside.

Most of the time I am not aware of the height of my secure bastion. I might just as well be on the ground in a tent. It is only when I peek out at the falling rain that I sometimes gasp at my precarious position, sharing a space with the surrounding giant trees that dwarf my pitiful existence. However, nothing yet has dampened my enthusiasm.

My writing goes well but I ache from sleeping in a sleeping bag on the bare floor. I will have my ground crew buy one of those egg crate, sponge rubber, mattress pads for me.

So far I have dedicated my time to a couple of short stories. The strange thing is, that being up here, I feel very remote from the things I am attempting to write about. It is as though I have removed myself from the everyday cares and concerns of the people in my stories. I am very much alone, and perhaps this aloneness influences my feelings about my characters and their picayune lives. Up here I seem to have the feeling that our struggles down below are indeed small and of little import. I now realize that my recent irritations are that way, although at the time they seemed all-consuming and vitally important.

Naturally, I have become extremely introspective and with the kind of gloomy atmosphere of my shelter I find that it is difficult to maintain a gaiety of spirit. This lends a definite saturnine flavor to my writing. I shall have to discipline myself so that this dour attitude does not defeat my purpose in being up here.

I wanted to be alone and I still do. I want to give whatever creative ability I have the best possible opportunity to express itself without the negative effects of the society in which I am forced to live. However, it now occurs to me that perhaps I have only succeeded in constructing another environment, equally oppressive, in yet another dimension. I shall have to stay the course to see if I am damned no matter what direction I choose. It may also be that my "creative ability" is nothing but a farce to begin with. In which case I shall simply resign myself to the ranks of the obscure and uninteresting, and there console myself with the works of people who have something to say, and a bottle of good Scotch.

I wish I had brought a book or two with me. Reading someone else's work might give me some inspiration. I remember reading Emile Zola's *Germaine* and it so inspired me that I went out trying to find some poor people to write about. I couldn't find any and if I had what would I have written about them. That's the trouble, you have to write about what you know, and although my family was poor during the Great Depression, I didn't know it. I thought that was the way the world was all the time. I had a great time growing up. I never felt poor. I grew up thinking shoes were made with holes in the bottoms. No. Not really.

The best joke I ever heard about growing up poor was, when asked, "how poor were you?" the man questioned responded, "If I didn't wake up with an erection in the morning I had nothing to play with all day long." Now *that's* poor.

Day 4.

"…sitting there like a pig to war."

—My Mother

❦   ❦   ❦

I was just thinking that my mother, if she were still alive, would have had strong objections regarding this latest insanity of mine. She would have joined with my wife and the two of them would have picked on me mercilessly until I'd have either given up or run away. Probably the latter, and to the nearest bar.

Once I got up here my mother would have said, "There you are sitting up there like a pig to war." That was one of her many expressions that I never really understood. Another was "It's not what you want that makes you fat." I always supposed that those expressions meant something to someone but I'm not sure to this day.

I think the first observation about the pig to war probably came from the Napoleonic Wars where the armies would take livestock with them in carts to wherever the fighting was. I've read about this in history books, and I suppose the pigs sat in the carts as happy as a pig can get, about going for a ride in the country. So I imagine that the reference is to some imbecile sitting where it is unlikely for him to be, happy to be there, and unaware of his impending doom. A real ninny. That's what she'd think about me sitting up here.

As to the other saying, I can only assume that it means it's not what you want but what you *eat* that makes you fat. That's about as close as I can come.

My folks had a lot of old sayings that they would pull out of their memory banks whenever the occasion warranted it. Quite a few were for my benefit at times when I was in trouble over something. Most of them I understood, like,

"You can't dress up a pig," or, "One boy is a whole boy, two boys are half a boy, and three boys are no boy at all."

Those were understandable enough but always sounded a little like code to me. I was never sure how to respond to these indirect accusations. They usually just made me squirm.

Day 5.

"…Methinks thou dost protest too much."

—Shakespeare

❧   ❧   ❧

I thought of not writing in my journal today. I couldn't think of anything to write, which is extremely unusual for me. Ordinarily I can dredge up a thought or two or a hundred to talk about. I'm very verbose when you come right down to it. However, I like to think that I'm interesting to listen to even though my wife doesn't always agree. It's probably that she has heard all my stories too many times. But then that's just one of the trials of marriage. Someone's got to do the story telling and someone has to roll her eyes to the heavens.

It rains continually and I have to keep my tarpaulin pulled down all around my platform. I don't feel too good, every joint I have aches without letup. Sleeping on the hard platform (the egg crate helps some), and not getting any exercise is beginning to tell on me. I will have to do something to alleviate my discomfort. It is even affecting my writing.

It seems the media has already forgotten me. In messages my wife sends me when I need food, she tells me that I haven't been mentioned in the press or on TV in the last couple of days. That's good because for the first few days there were many people, curiosity seekers, and some tree huggers, that came just to see an old man up a tree. Even they don't come now. It's funny how quickly things pass. We all live our lives in the here and now, and yesterday has little significance once we have moved on.

Does anyone ever think seriously about continuity? I doubt it. But the thought occurred to me that I have broken the continuity of my life. I have purposely removed myself from the contiguous routine of living. Not that my life was the universal routine of rising, getting dressed, eating breakfast, going to work, eating lunch, going back to work, going home, eating dinner, watching TV, going to bed, only to do it again the next day. After all, I'm retired, but I did have a routine, one where I got up, had coffee while I read the newspaper, went for my morning walk, came home, showered, etc., and then either paid bills, did some writing, ran errands, whatever. Not a particularly spectacular beginning to the day but then show me someone that has a spectacular beginning and I'll show you a spectacular nincompoop.

Now, being up here, I've completely abandoned my routine and in so doing sacrificed my continuity. This brought me to the realization that we humans need continuity. It is the thing upon which we can count, in which we can believe. It is the foundation of our world. It is the thing which directs our course and by which we recognize ourselves.

By climbing up this tree (actually being hauled up), I have severed my uninterrupted connection with the things which characterize my being. I have, in short, dumped my lifetime scenario down the toilet. I have opted for a leap into the unknown and I am now convinced that I shall learn from the experience, but probably, I will pay dearly for it.

Day 6.

❦　　　❦　　　❦

I feel a little depressed and maybe a little lonely today. I'm not a social animal. I don't have many close friends anymore, (they insist on dying), and I don't go out of my way to make new ones. It's a flaw in my character. Therefore, I write, and the writing does externalize my thoughts and feelings to some degree. I don't know what I'd do otherwise.

I know I've suffered on and off from depression all my life, nothing severe enough or too prolonged for it to be called chronic. However, it's always been there.

I've developed a kind of theory about it. I think most people suffer from it at times, probably more than they're willing to admit even if they recognize it as depression. It's a kind of existential sickness that afflicts the human race. We all suffer from it, this sickness, this aloneness, but most of us manage to keep ourselves so busy with our diversions, work, play, getting and spending, that we keep it from taking us over.

I think a lot of it comes from the no-win situation we find ourselves in from the day that we become aware of death. We know we can't win. We're all going to die and the knowledge of death is like a virus that we carry with us every day, all the time, and it makes a mockery of all of our endeavors. However, that same knowledge also lightens our lifetime burdens because we know it will all end one day. As Shakespeare had one of his characters say in one of his plays, I think it was in *Henry IV*, "By my troth I care not, a man can die but once, we owe God a death, and let it go which way it will, he who dies this year is quit for the next."

It has occurred to me that a lot of the great creative people in the world, composers, artists, writers, were depressives. Some of these people were barely sane because of their depression.

Once upon a time, in one of my fits of depression, I composed what I then thought was the perfect epitaph, it's in Latin and goes: *Id erat vastus magni temperus*, which liberally translated means, "This has been a big waste of time."

Of course, I don't really feel that way.

I wrote a poem today. It seems that the only time I write poetry is when I'm depressed. Anyway, it goes like this:

Time and life,

Those grand conspirators,

Are making me old.

I feel worn and tamed,

By all this life,

This coming and going,

This certain knowledge

Of beginnings and endings,

Of obvious results

From predictable actions.

Through some peep-hole in this universe,

I peer through timeworn eyes

Into the space of my own reality,

Beholding a narrow band of light,

The years of my being,

Bordered on either side by darkness.

Looking deeply, the light becomes a magic pool,

Reflecting the colored shadows

Of places and faces,

The swimming motion of a thousand lives,

Manifesting, undulating,

Evaporating in a vapor of time,
Consumed by the dark.

Day 7.

"I should have been a pair of ragged claws
Scuttling across the floors of silent seas."

—T. S. Eliot

❧   ❧   ❧

I've been wondering what the hell I'm doing up here. It just dawned on me that aside from my few meager comforts all I have with me is me, and what's in my head. I don't have books or TV or informational disks for my laptop. That thought struck me as a very lonely idea. I'm the only company I have and I'm beginning to wonder if I am a suitable companion for myself. Have I lost perspective?

I realized that we are all very much alone. When we are deprived of all socialization, our work, our daily activities, all of our diversions, our busyness, as I am, we are truly alone. Or, is it that we are always truly alone and it is just our constant motion that keeps us from realizing it? Now that I have stopped everything except breathing, I realize just how alone I am. I have voluntarily isolated myself to pursue some peace and quiet, but now I find that I am forced to rely on myself as the only person in my world, and it's damned lonely.

I don't mean to be existential but I can't help seeing myself and, for that matter everyone, as single individuals encased within a physical skin and another type of skin made up of beliefs and a peculiar psychological personality. This being alone is doing funny things to my brain.

There was a wonderful line in the movie *Blazing Saddles* that I think may fit my present circumstance. In the movie, at a town meeting everyone agrees to hire a new sheriff to counter the bad guys who make living in the town most unpleasant. At the end of the meeting, the preacher who presided, entreats the Divine Being with the words, "Oh, Lord, is this really thy will, or are we just jerking off?" As applied to me I wonder, not about the Lord's will, but my own, and if I am "just jerking off?"

Getting back to only me being in this tree. The fact that I am my single source of information, stimulus, excitement, or intelligence is a disquieting thought. I am my one companion and what is stored in my brain is my sole resource. I am my entire universe and what I know is everything there is for I have no access to anything outside my universe.

I may go mad.

Day 8.

"Why don't you come up and see me sometime?"

—Mae West

❦   ❦   ❦

I remember my grandson had a fantasy friend when he was very young. He called this friend of his "Ockiteck." Ockiteck was endowed with magical pow-ers, and was also funny, and talkative, and a perfectly enjoyable companion. Why not? We all have alter egos and perhaps I can create my own Ockiteck and endow him with all the virtues, intelligence, and volubility that I desire in a comrade. Since I am lord of my universe I don't see why I can't do anything I like. I'll give it a try.

I composed this Pogo-type poem just for the fun of it. It's full of poignant pithiness.

Here I sit all filled with ennui,
Looking forward fondly
To the days that used to be,
Pondering the whys,
And even the wherefore,
And finding there a lot of not,
And a bit of neither-nor.

Speaking of Mae West, I adored her, although she was somewhat before my time. She was definitely a sex symbol and I have always had a distinct liking for women who admitted to being women and sexually liberated. She exhibited the kind of honest and ribald sensuality that I admire in anyone. Let's face it we're all sexual creatures. Why not admit it and let it go at that.

Sex is such a big deal because we make it that way. It's a kind of game we play. We have made it such a big taboo because a long time ago our puritan ancestors proclaimed that sex was only acceptable under conditions of matrimony and then only for purposes of procreation. We all know that is so much bullshit. Our puritan forebears were probably the greatest hypocrites in the history of mankind, but a lot of their ersatz beliefs still bother our consciences in some parts of society. Those stupid beliefs make liars, cheats, and guilty sinners of us all.

Anthropologists tell us that we are the only animals that have sex randomly and just for fun. All the other mammals only have sex when the female ovulates and is in a condition to conceive. God, I'm glad I'm human.

Day 9.

❧   ❧   ❧

My Ockiteck and I have had several pleasant conversations on a variety of subjects: family, sex, Chaos Theory, memory and memories, truth, freedom, beliefs, sacrifice, religion, politics, history, and a host of other questions and concepts. I may record some of these conversations, maybe not the conversations themselves but the condensed results of them. Sounds like it might inspire me to start writing again.

My wife and daughter have bought themselves a bullhorn and insist on bull horning up their questions and concerns about my health, and when am I coming down, and every other nonsensical thing they can think of. They stand at the bottom of my tree and talk to me through this devil's megaphone until I get fed up and tell them to shut up and go away. I'm not acting very nice but then I came up here to get away from people, even my own family, for a short time, and I still insist on doing it.

One thing that Ockiteck and I talked about is one of my favorite subjects, Chaos Theory. It derived from a meteorologist who couldn't figure out why he couldn't predict the weather with any accuracy more than three days in advance. He finally concluded that the weather forecasters only take into account the big things that affect the weather like the jet stream, the movement of fronts, upper and lower atmosphere winds and storms and so forth. They never consider the little more unpredictable things like the effects of topogra-phy, the amount of reflection from the "Heaviside layer," or the effects of cloud cover on temperature and precipitation. Well, it seems these things are very difficult to take into account in the overall movement of weather and, there-fore, can skew the weather in innumerable ways so that predictions further out than three days are highly questionable.

The theory became popular in the entire scientific community to explain any number of things, such as improper answers, or repeated experiments that should always yield the same results but do not. In the field of mathematics, for example, it seems that all mathematicians deal primarily with linear equations, these are the biggies and the simplest to solve. The mathematicians always come very close to the correct answer to any given problem by solving these linear equations. However, inherent in many, if not all problems are some nig-gling little irritants called non-linear equations that keep mathematicians from absolutely divining the absolute answer to these problems. As I understand it these non-linear equations are pesky little varmints and are very difficult to solve.

Now, I really don't know what the hell I'm talking about but I read a book one time about Chaos Theory and it really impressed me. I started relating it to human behavior and all of the minor happenstances that seem to underlie our existence. I wonder if we even recognize these seemingly insignificant incidents in our lives that keep us from ever achieving our goals or even true happiness.

Such small things as not getting a good night's sleep, and as a result being somewhat of a grouch the following day, which causes an alienation of affec-tion from one's spouse or children or boss or coworkers and maybe leading to a conflict that otherwise would not have happened. Of course, this scenario could go on and on, and balloon into a life-shattering series of incidents, but we needn't go that far.

One of the best examples of Chaos Theory influencing our lives is the daily fluctuation in the stock market where small, almost insignificant events such as the failure of one company to meet its quarterly dividend projection can turn the market down dramatically. The ramification of that downturn has equally dramatic effects on other stocks, bonds, futures, retirement accounts, and so on. A good example of Chaos at work.

The national economy itself is another good example. We live and die in a plethora of good and bad news. Minor changes in production or labor costs or the cost of a barrel of oil can have a severe effect on an economy so precari-ously balanced as ours. How about the dive in profit margins for U. S. companies because of imports from the Pacific Rim countries, Mexico, Central and South America? It all had to start somewhere and once it did it became a landslide to what it is now: a boon for consumers and anathema to U. S. producers.

Then, of course, we have government. How can any system survive the Chaos that exists in government? Our government and, for that matter, all governments in the world have built-in "Murphy's Law" clauses that clearly prevent anything from ever going smoothly. Government is the perfect proving ground for Chaos Theory because the small, unforeseen, iniquitous, ambiguous imperfections inherent in government prove that no matter how carefully a system is put together the little imperfections will ultimately overwhelm it.

My point is that small, insignificant, non-linear factors can have a deleterious effect on our lives without us ever realizing it. It does make a person wonder. Doesn't it?

Day 10.

❧   ❧   ❧

Thinking about family led me to write something down. Ockiteck and I had a conversation about this just last night. It went something like this:

I seem to think a lot about my childhood and the people and things I grew up with. Not long ago, after hearing of another death of an old time movie star, I felt like I had lost someone near and dear to me. I felt as though one of my family had died and that sent me off thinking about what family really is.

I grew up at a time in the world when a lot was happening, not that there isn't a lot happening all the time, but in those days the great depression was beginning, Hitler was gaining power in Germany, the arts and sciences were exploding all over the world, literature was perhaps at its pinnacle (at least in America), music was being produced at a prodigious rate, and Hollywood was at its zenith with more legitimate "Stars" than at any other time in its history, then and now. I grew up in the midst of all of these things, they were all part of me, even the most remote of them.

My conclusion is that these people, the good and the bad, were all part of my family. They had as direct an influence on my life as did my mother and father, indeed, sometimes I think more so. In addition, when one of them dies I lose someone close to me and I am the less for it. John Donne said it–"Each man's death diminishes me, for I am involved in mankind; wherefore never seek to ask for whom the bell tolls, it tolls for thee."

Then came the sticky part for if I adopt this definition of family then I am forced to go further. Were all of the people in the world during my lifetime "my family," the Nazis, the Jews, the leaders of nations, the soldiers in all the wars, all the good and bad guys the world over?

I had to search within myself to answer the question and this is what I thought: All of the people, far and near did indeed influence me and possibly make my life what it has been. Oh, I know that genes predestined me to some extent, perhaps, far more than we suspect, but the world we are born into and grow up in may be far more influential than any predisposition coming from our chemistry.

I seem to have a built-in understanding and compassion for those people who preceded me in the years prior to my birth. Somehow my empathy extends far more toward them than it does with the younger generations of today. Perhaps, this is typical of old age. I have trouble identifying with young people with orange hair and pierced tongues and lips, (how do they kiss?). However, this empathy for older generations is something in my gut, not explainable by rational means, except maybe that it is something I gained by association with my family and the generation of which I was a part.

Still, I wonder at it. I was not aware I was absorbing so much knowledge and more than knowledge, so much awareness of what the world was feeling. I was not even slightly aware of how the impending war in Europe was invading my thoughts and conditioning my behavior. I knew I loved the movies and the heroes and the drama of the stories. But I did not identify any of these people as close to me, as part of my family, even though I was deeply influenced by them and the fictitious or real life dramas in which they acted. It has taken me all this time to begin to recognize that.

What is the definition of family anyway? I think it goes way beyond what the dictionary says. I think it must be closer to: Family—the entire group of people into which one is born and that group which immediately precedes and succeeds that person.

Where does one stop with that definition? How much of history has conditioned our time and consequently, us? Certainly, we must say all of it. Therefore is our family all of the human race? Are we all allied together? Are we all, as members of the same family, responsible for all of the good and bad the world has ever known? In my own case was I part of the evil in the world at the time of the Holocaust? Were the Nazis my brothers, only in a different context, in another part of the world? Was I a Jew by another name and a victim as much as they? Was I the predator and the prey, not only then, but all through history? I am inclined to think so, but one has to go far beyond himself and our tiny allocation of space and time to encompass such a theory. Interesting questions.

These strange rumblings in my soul
Arise from what unquiet spring,
To seep and swell,
And form the tides that surge and fret,
And nurture wanderings.

My spirit takes no shape,
But lingers as the wind,
Across a vast and vacant sea,
Seeking, as the waves, the shore.

Day 11.

"A strong memory is generally coupled
with an infirm judgment."

—Montaigne

❦　　　❦　　　❦

I've been reminiscing a lot over the past few days. Seems I've been doing more thinking than writing and that's okay but I don't want to neglect the writing. I've been thinking that maybe what I started out to write is not all that satisfying and the writing isn't that good, but I'll keep on. What else do I have to do?

Maybe I need to write more about what I'm thinking and talking to Charlie about. By the way, I gave my Ockiteck a name. It was too awkward to refer to him as Ockiteck. Why I picked the name Charlie is anybody's guess. Maybe because of Steinbeck's last book *Travels With Charlie.* Of course, in that case Charlie was a dog, and who knows, maybe my Charlie is Steinbeck's Charlie in another incarnation. Ha! That's a dandy. How can a fantasy character be an incarnation, but then again why not? We may all be fantasy incarnations in the mind of God.

At the conclusion of all my reminiscing, of course, I wrote a poem. I can't help myself. It's a flaw in my character.

How still the voices of my past,
How long since they have stirred my soul,
And filled my mind
With longing for the world
Outside myself.

I am time-withered now.
I've reached and passed
A hundred crossroads,
Survived, accepted,
Compromised, conformed,
And, at last succeeded
In conquering what once
I was, in all my dreams.

Time has tricked me grievously,
I've had to do with practicality,
I've fought each day with detail,
Labored hard to satisfy
The day's requirement,
Put down my wild impetuosity,
And written off my dreams
As folly.

I will excuse myself now, my abandoned wife is on that damnable bullhorn again, and I have to tell her I'm all right, and no, I haven't had a bowel movement yet.

Day 12.

"...and a time to every purpose under the heaven..."

—Ecclesiastes

❖   ❖   ❖

This thing about bowel movements is more serious than one might think. I have not been eating that much but still not having a BM for eight days is somewhat disconcerting. I am so full of crap that it's a wonder my blue eyes haven't turned brown.

Anyway, I have to use a fancy enameled bucket, I think they used to call them, "Slop Jars," and it is not a nice relaxing way to relieve one's self. So I usually pee over the side of the platform, I regard that as an act of returning some of the nutrients I have ingested back to the earth. I love that aspect of recycling. I think of it as the law of the conservation of matter that states that nothing is ever created or destroyed, it simply changes form.

However, back to my BMs. As I said, it has been eight days since my last one, and I have a full and uncomfortable feeling in my lower bowels. I've thought of asking my wife to send up some sort of laxative, but then the thought of using that damned bucket to where it was nigh unto overflowing so offends my esthetic senses that I go another day without relief.

I have thought that instead of using my bucket I would simply hang my butt over the side of the platform and let fly. Of course, I would have to rig some sort of safety harness to keep from falling but I could do that. However, the mental picture I have of me all harnessed up, with nothing but my feet still on the platform and my bare butt hanging out in space, while my wife waits expectantly below, is one I simply cannot contemplate without doubling up in a loud and boisterous guffaw.

Day 13.

"...for there is nothing good or bad
but thinking makes it so."

—Shakespeare

🍁　　　🍁　　　🍁

Charlie, talk to me.

I'm right with you.

I think you are my dark side.

I am the counter to your point?

Yes, my alter ego, my other half, my balance.

I'm that anyway.

Yeah, I guess you are.

Whether you like it or not, I'm always with you. Wherever you are, there I am.

We are.

If you prefer to think of me as a separate entity.

Somehow it keeps things straighter that way. I can state my opinion on anything and then you jump in with a counter argument. It helps to keep me from going all the way overboard. It keeps me from being a die-hard conservative and also from being a goddamned bleeding heart liberal.

I serve a valuable service.

Yes you do. You know in the Sung or Chung or Chin dynasty there were two schools of philosophical thought, which is kind of what you and I have going. One school maintained that man is intrinsically evil and only society turns him into a somewhat acceptable human being. Whereas, the other school thought that man is inherently good and society corrupts him.

Which school do you belong to?

I have to think that man is a son-of-a-bitch to begin with. Look at all the babies in the world, if you can spread your vision that far, they are inherently selfish, greedy, demanding, mean spirited, totally dependent, loud, filthy in their personal habits, and to anyone except their mother (and sometimes not even to her), aggravating, messy, noisy, little bundles of confined energy insisting on constant attention and comforting.

I'm sure every mother in the world will be happy to hear that message.

Let me finish. Therefore, with that ugly beginning it takes years of concentrated training to turn that baby into a tolerable creature. And, from the ages of about four to maybe twelve the child can be, if not pleasurable, at least bearable. Then comes the worst possible period in a parent's life, puberty—teenage-hood. God, spare us all.

Up to that point society has tried its best to take that lump of clay called "the little darling" and turn it into a somewhat decent beginning human being. However, when teenage-hood strikes there is little one can do, short of execution, except exile them to a boarding school or a Military Academy or a foreign country.

What pleasure you must have taken seeing your own children grow up. I suppose you felt the way you just expressed with your own young.

No. You're right. When they're your own you feel differently. It's a flaw in Mother Nature's character. Did I ever tell you my solution for successfully raising kids? No? Then allow me. My idea is that as soon as possible you put them in a large barrel and feed them through the bunghole. When they get to the first sign of teenage-hood you plug up the bunghole. Simple, huh?

God, you're good. An inspiration for prospective parents.

Speaking of prospective parents. There are only two outstanding activities that mankind is good at. One is making babies and the other is killing one another. There's point and counterpoint for you.

Making babies isn't a bad thing.

Oh no? First of all I think most babies are accidents. They're just the by-products of fucking, (notice I didn't say making love), and you will never stop people fucking. Secondly, if young people were adequately informed about babies and children, and the fact that they sign up for a 20-year (or more) contract with each child, maybe they might take having a child more seriously. Thirdly, the world is overpopulated now and if all the people in the world continue fucking and making babies and the babies, when grown, make more babies, pretty soon we're going to be up to our eyebrows in babies, smell, and all.

So, would you turn yours back in if you had the chance?

No, I suppose not.

End of argument.

Day 14.

"...with small flags waving and tinny blasts on tiny trumpets,
we may meet the enemy, and not only may he be ours,
he may be us."

—Walt Kelly

❦   ❦   ❦

I'm feeling better. I started doing isometric exercises and also some stretching exercises for about 10 minutes twice a day and it's made a considerable difference in my overall condition. The rain stopped for almost a whole day yesterday and I pulled back the drapes and gloried in the warm sunshine. I was not alone, all around me it seemed all the world woke from its continual bath and sprung to life, the birds, the insects, the foliage, even the big trees seemed to thrill to the sun.

My writing has slowed to a trickle. I think it's because I started doubting what it was I was putting into words. Some words bother me tremendously, words like, always or never, or should, or would, or could, and the biggies like, truth, and honor, and the biggest of all, reality. I get hung up on words like these because they are so illusive, so subjective, and they cannot be trusted to convey the intention of the writer.

These doubts I have concern just that. I know what I try to say but it is from my viewpoint, my subjective reality, how I perceive the world, and not only is that extremely difficult to communicate but by the time it is filtered through the reader's mind what of the original intent is left? I was so concerned about this that, naturally, I had to write a small insignificant essay about it. I call it:

VARIATION ON A THEME BY HOWARD COSSELL

Howard Cossell, one of America's most controversial sports commentators, had one favorite phrase, that he never failed to use at least once in every one of his usually malignant diatribes indicting some sports figure for ignominious and inconsequential behavior. The phrase was: "Telling it like it is." He forgot to add that it was, "Telling it like it is," from Howard Cossell's perspective. How strange that he believed that his perspective was reality and that he was the sole agent of the "Truth."

This business of truth is extremely tricky. Truth may be said to be only extant in science and that only because an experiment is repeatable. I don't know if that constitutes truth or not. It may only prove that an experiment is repeatable.

In the realm of individual opinion, truth is an illusion. It is a "fact" only through the perception and reaction of an individual to certain apparent circumstances. The old saw that opinions are like noses, everybody's got one, is closer to truth than any opinion expressed by those who have noses.

The fact of the matter is that we each exist in our own personal reality. Moreover, that reality is colored by our genetic structure and our current and past environmental conditioning. Physically, we don't even see colors the same way, we don't think the same way, we don't have the same nervous systems, or neural pathways in our brains, or taste, smell, touch, or hear in an identical manner. In effect we are all isolated by our physical, mental, and emotional makeup, and we live in a reality which is entirely of our own making.

We do, however, have many general considerations of reality that are common. Most of us can distinguish red from green at stoplights. Most of us recognize the same concepts of physical existence, such as the necessity to eat, to earn a living, to obey some semblance of civil behavior, and to endorse the general boundaries of the society of which we are a part. However, that does not include our innermost thoughts, or feelings, those are peculiarly our own, and spring from our own perception of reality.

We give a lot of credence to the external aspects of our lives, such as our job, and even tend to define ourselves by what we do rather than what we are. However, behind our self-made facade there exists an internal perception of ourselves, our beliefs, and our reality. Moreover, we are at the center of that reality because each of us is our own universe. We view the world through the ability of our five senses, our belief systems, and our physical, mental, and emotional acuity. To us that is reality.

There are other belief systems that hold that what we know as reality, personal or otherwise, is nothing but illusion. That reality is something we cannot conceive because behind the reality we see is far more in micro and macro than we can imagine. Science is proving this to us daily. Life is so much more than we can experience with our limited perception. We are miniscule when compared to that which exists.

However, here we are, at this nexus of space and time and we can do no more than what we are doing, even though, like Howard Cossell, we may believe we have the only true insight into the workings of the world and the people in it, and as a superior person we should be free to criticize anyone and everyone. On the other hand should we be more aware of our insignificance, and perhaps, more generous in our view of mankind?

The world has progressed to exactly where it is by whatever means and pathways, and although it is imperfect in our eyes, it just may be precisely where we should be. In any case we will all do what we will do, rightly, wrongly, or otherwise, and the world will continue in its elliptical meandering around an insignificant star for a very long time, with us or without. And that's, "telling it like it is."

Day 15.

"Deck us all with Boston Charlie,
Fa, la, la, la, la,—la, la, la, la,
Nora's sleeping on the trolley,
Fa, la, la, la, la,—la, la, la, la."

—Walt Kelley—POGO (sung to the tune of Deck the Halls)

❧   ❧   ❧

I have begun feeling much better in the past few days. I am exercising regularly and I have restored my potty habits almost to normal. I gave up the idea of the harness and crapping in space. It was not a practical idea. Besides if by chance there was a tourist or better yet, a reporter, down below and accidentally got hit with flying feces, I am sure I would be castigated in every magazine from The New Yorker to National Geographic as a menace to society at large and a particularly dangerous example for our youth. Maybe, if I were sure it was a reporter down below, I'd do it anyway, and the devil take all the people who would forego seeing the pleasure in it.

How come there is so little humor left in the world? I love to laugh. I think most people do but we sure find it difficult to have something to laugh about these days. The comic strips are not even as funny as they used to be. Has the world grown more serious?

I think people are the funniest things in the world. And the best thing of all is when we can laugh at ourselves. I guess that's why I loved POGO so much. Even though Walt Kelly portrayed us in costumes of swamp animals, the message came through loud and strong. He saw the humor in our everyday concerns and anxieties, our longings, our innocent comings and goings, and our striving to make drama out of our ludicrous egos. I loved it. In my mind he is one of the greatest twentieth century philosophers. He saw us as we are, at our comical, ridiculous best, trying earnestly all the while to take life and ourselves seriously.

I think it all comes from how we define ourselves. I see myself, in my mind, as I was at age 35. Young, healthy, good looking, and able to leap tall buildings at a single bound. That's the mental image I have of myself that I carry with me all the time. It is a terrible shock when I bother to look in a mirror, which I try not to do too often. It is equally terrible when I try to do something physical that is now beyond my capability. I hate that.

But, getting back to my point, (that's another thing, I seem to keep losing my points), how do we define ourselves? I used to define myself by saying I was a Management Consultant but that wasn't me. That wasn't what I was or am. That's what I did when I used to work for a living. So, how do I define myself now? I say I'm retired. That's just another way of saying what I do. Is what we do what we are?

In *Twenty Years After*, Alexandre Dumas has d'Artagnan say, "He not only knows you by your name, but by your deeds." Perhaps, that is the definition of a person—their deeds. I have also heard it said: Tell me what your passions are; tell me what you love, and I will know you. That sounds closer to what a person is instead of what one does. I think it would be very nice to meet people on the basis of what interests them most, what their passion is, and what it is that they love. But then people are hesitant about exposing themselves in that manner. It takes a long time to get to know a person that well. We all might be a little more understanding if we knew those things about each other.

Day 16.

❦   ❦   ❦

Speaking of youth, and my being a dangerous example or, for that matter any kind of example, who the hell cares? Why, I would like to ask, are we so hung up on youth? Instead, why aren't we hung up on intelligence, ability, or virtue? Why can't we endorse a system of discipline, courtesy, manners, proper behavior, and respect for those older and wiser than one's self? Whatever happened to those old fashioned ideas? Why have we let children take over the responsibility for raising themselves and reduced parents to the role of provider and servant?

Personally, I'm all in favor of Universal Military Training for all boys AND girls. If nothing more it may train them how to say, "Yes sir," and maybe, "Thank you," and "You're welcome," instead of "Yo," "Dude," and "No problem." God, our society has diminished in so many ways.

When I was a child, it was the adults who conversed; children listened. And woe to any child that presumed equal status and interrupted an adult conversation. Moreover, you know what? That generation raised courteous, well mannered, and respectful children into courteous, well mannered, and respectful adults. See? It can be done.

What a disservice we do to our children when we let them lead the way. When we voluntarily transfer the power that is rightfully and responsibly ours to children who have no training, no discipline, little intellect, and no experience. What are we thinking? We not only betray our children, ourselves, and society but we are conditioning generations of young people, that otherwise could become mature and sensible adults, into selfish, materialistic, unthinking, perpetual adolescents.

Another thing, with this overwhelming preoccupation with youth, and the obsession with making them safe from child molesters, predatory priests, teachers, and virtually all men, we have created a society where we are afraid of our own children. I won't even walk by a schoolyard for fear one of the kids will report me as a dirty old man watching children on the playground. I used to like kids and took pleasure in watching them play together; observe their joy, and enthusiasm. It allowed me to think back to my own childhood, and for a moment relive being young again.

I don't do that anymore. I'd be arrested.

Day 17.

"This above all to thine own self be true…"

—Shakespeare

❦   ❦   ❦

I started thinking about truth again. What is truth? Is there such a thing? Or is truth so subjective that it is at best illusory, at worst a lie. I seem to remember in one of Shakespeare's Sonnets a line that goes: "Most true it is, that I have looked on truth askance and strangely…" I must admit that I do so now.

I think that truth is unachievable because hidden in what one person calls "truth" is a subterfuge of that person's ego, knowledge, perception, and agenda. One man's truth is another man's cold succotash. It is personal and mostly likely it is not truth at all.

So if there is no truth then how can we be certain of anything? What will constitute our reality without truth? How can we make the distinction of good and evil without truth?

Truth is generally defined as "fact" or "reality" but whose "facts" and whose "reality"? If all is truly subjective then fact or reality is each person's judgment of those relative perceptions. And if that is the case then can "truth" truly exist?

The only possible exception is mathematics and I suspect that the further a person penetrates into the world of math the more questionable that "truth" becomes.

Of course, two plus two will always equal four. And I guess you can call that truth. I call it arithmetic. I am speaking of philosophical truth and I challenge anyone to prove to me that it does indeed exist. And, maybe it doesn't matter a whit if it does.

Don't ask me. I don't have the answers. All I can seem to do is pose the questions.

Day 18.

"But nothing could ever daunt him, or overcome, for a moment, his habitual good humor."

—Dana

❧   ❧   ❧

Things go along. Will this damnable rain ever stop? I should have known it would be this way. I checked out all the weather information and statistics I could find before coming up here and I should have known that 100 inches of rain per year translates to slightly over a quarter of an inch per day, and because it is mostly delivered as a slow drizzle that leaves very damn little time for the sun to shine. Ah, well, the rain and the fog keep me inside and closed up so that the only thing I can do is converse with Charlie, and write down our most consummate conclusions to share with the world. Yeah, right!

We had a nice discussion last evening concerning humor. It crops up everywhere and some of the funniest stuff never gets spread around and appreciated. Therefore, Charlie had me write down some of the funny stuff I could remember and there was so much of it I distilled it down to a few vignettes and stories that didn't require lengthy explanations of the circumstances involved in creating the humor. I'll write some of these down so I don't forget them.

In a subway restroom in New York City, I saw this graffiti on the wall in front of the urinal I was using at the time:

(The first person wrote): God is dead—Nietzsche

(The second person wrote): Nietzsche is dead—God
(The third person wrote): God is alive and living in Argentina

Here's a limerick:

There was a buxom young lass from Milpitas, (really, it's in California),
Who was overly fond of coitus,
Till a half-back from State made her period late,
And now she's got athlete's fetus.

Memorable bumper stickers:

Fight the war on poverty; throw a hand grenade at a beggar.

Advice:

Beware of people who drive while talking on a cell phone. Not only may they have the phone in their ear, they may have their head up their ass.

Don't have babies unless you have a plan, and included in that plan should be a prohibition against having babies.

To test who your real friends are, break both your arms, and find out who will help you pee.

Never trust friendly bankers, teenagers who swear they don't drink or have sex, TV ads, what you read in the newspapers, or anything having the label "New and Improved."

If you have a hunch about something don't let "common sense" override it.

If marriage scares the hell out of you, don't let your best man or bride's maid talk the hell back into you.

Don't bare your soul to anyone; you'll look foolish unclothed.

Music is a safe haven for the overworked or overwrought.

Don't get agitated standing in a line at a checkout station, let those ahead of you expend their energy on impatience. You can watch.

Take your wife roses.

Day 19.

"They clear away vast masses of oppressive gravity by their sense of the ridiculous, which is at bottom a combination of sound moral judgment with lighthearted good."

—Nietzsche

❦　　　❦　　　❦

Over the years I have had some pretty outrageous friends. I seem to have peculiar tastes in almost everything. I like strong-willed women; men, who in some way are characters or mavericks; strong booze; true literature; classical music; jazz; dogs and horses. These friends I mentioned were truly uncivilized. Most of them were heavy drinkers, unfaithful to their wives, not good fathers, and would rather promote nonsense than adherence to authority and the "establishment." These friendships took place in the 1950s and the world was different then. Although I have met a few good friends since who share my love of the unholy and my dislike of the urbane phonies of the world.

Friends like that are really the only people I care to know. They are interesting and, if you're lucky, may have something of importance to say. These are the only people one can learn something from. I often get the feeling that the world is populated by people who don't think very deeply.

Back in the Fifties, (when I was young, I might add), none of the crowd I ran with took life very seriously. We were very good at nonsense and devoted a lot of our time to it. We were fond of lampooning the company we all worked for at the time by circulating very official-looking memoranda concerning such important topics as the amount of time allowed in the restrooms; strict rules about fraternization with members of the opposite sex; the despicable habit of nose-picking while at work; the prohibition against enjoying your work and laughter in general; and the absolute forbiddance of writing ersatz and frivolous memos.

Nothing, but nothing was sacrosanct or unassailable. The more revered a subject, the more it was ridiculed and derided by vicious rapscallions bent on reducing the matter to its ultimate insignificance. This of course included religion, especially Catholicism (Mackerel Snappers); Christian Science (Faith Healers); and protestants of any and all denominations, each having related disparaging descriptors.

That reminds me of another limerick that was dedicated to a lovely young woman who was a Christian Scientist.

> There was a Faith Healer from Kiel,
> Who said, "Though pain is not real,
> When I sit on a pin
> And it punctures the skin
> I dislike what I fancy I feel."

Oh, for the fun days of youth when one is immortal; life is a hoot; and all's well with the world.

Day 20.

❧   ❧   ❧

Thinking about liking horses got me off on another tangent, that of possessions. A horse is a possession but you have to wonder who possesses whom. A horse is a heavy responsibility. In a lot of ways a horse is like a baby. You have to feed it, bathe it, exercise it, tend to its medical requirements, trim its hooves, and even be responsible for its conduct. It is no small job.

This line of reasoning led me to the fact that all of our possessions incur a lot of obligations, time, and effort. I had a friend tell me that he spent three weeks of work on his boat to have it on the water for one week. He had to have it in a slip in a marina, which cost an arm and a leg to rent, he had to haul it out once a year to have its bottom scraped, he constantly had to paint it and varnish it and repair sails and rigging and for all of that he got to enjoy sailing it one week out of four, and then for only about four months out of the year. In addition, he had a lot of money invested which he probably will never recover.

Or, for example, take owning a cabin in the mountains or at the beach. Not only do you have the headache of maintenance on your expensive second domicile but you feel honor bound to use the damn thing every chance you get to justify the money you have invested in it. It literally dictates where you will vacation unless you're rich enough to let it sit idle waiting for the few times you may want to use it for a weekend.

Now take houses. Your home is the most expensive thing in your life. And, look at how much time and effort you spend just keeping it looking nice, let alone all the repair and basic maintenance it requires. Naturally, there is great benefit from it but the fact is that you spend a great deal of your time and money deriving that benefit. Then there are all of the accoutrements necessary for the good life inside your home. The appliances large and small, the furniture in every room, the several TVs, the sound system, the security system, the heating and air conditioning and humidifying systems, the computers and desks and books, and the overwhelming number of knickknacks, pictures, paintings, sculptures, clothes, cosmetics, dishes, canned goods, soft goods, frozen foods, and all manner of supplies that must be contained throughout the house. Additionally, one has to have the basement workshop with all of the power tools, and hand tools, and materials and supplies to allow you to do-it-yourself.

Then, of course, there are cars, and SUVs and house trailers, and motor homes and all of the equipage necessary to furnish and maintain those vehicles.

So on it goes, possessions on top of possessions until the house is nigh to exploding from this surplus of necessities and comforts and luxuries.

Aristotle once wrote that every citizen was justified in providing all the amenities one could afford to assure a comfortable life. I think Aristotle would be flabbergasted at what it takes to assure the modern American a comfortable life.

However, my question is do we own all of this stuff or does it own us? In many ways, such as in the case of a horse, or a boat, and, of course, a house, we are slave to the obligations we have undertaken on behalf of the animal or the unconscious but nonetheless demanding inanimate object or dwelling. In terms of expense and physical effort there can be no question that we are in servitude to these things, this stuff, these items of our, what? Greed?

There is an old Chinese saying that I have always remembered because it applied to me so well. It goes:

"It is a wise man who rids himself of the things which no longer serve him and which threaten to make him serve them." I think I have long ago passed the point where I could rid myself of those things. I have, most assuredly, become a slave to them.

However, I have shed all comforts and amenities up here in my high cocoon, and for the most part, I don't miss them, although a nice soft bed in the arms of my nice soft wife would sure be nice.

Day 21.

❧   ❧   ❧

The week before I took the leap up my tree. My wife and I went to a stage play. It was Tartuffe by Moliere and it was very good. The theater was filled with a mature audience with a lot of gray hair. There were no teenagers in attendance, nor even any twenty-somethings. We live in a university city and many of the attendees were academicians.

It got me to wondering about "culture." Of course, I'm familiar with the dictionary definition which says something like: enlightenment and excellence of taste acquired by intellectual and aesthetic acquaintance with and taste in fine arts, and the humanities. I like that: "enlightenment and excellence of taste." That's got to be the biggest line of bullshit I've ever heard.

Somehow I've always resented the arrogance inherent in the word "culture" and the people who claim to have it. I've had a rather plebeian education by most standards and I certainly don't maintain any illusion that I am one of the "cultured." However, I don't believe that attending plays, or symphonies, or dry lectures dedicated to the refined tastes of academicians, in any way con-tributes to my taste in fine arts, humanities, and the broad aspects of science. And, I pity the people who do.

I have known some very intelligent people whose knowledge of the world and the pragmatic aspects of life would put to shame all those who dwell in the illusory and hide-bound world of academia. They were not "cultured" people. In many cases they had little or no formal education but they *were truly* educated. Their lives had educated them and in the areas of literature and poetry and geography and mathematics and logic and morality and ethics they were comparable and even superior to many of the ersatz professors I had in college.

The old saw about "them that can, do; them that can't, teach," is, to my way of thinking, verifiable. I have very little use for professors and even less for preachers.

However, back to culture. I believe the most cultured people I have ever known are those whose honesty, integrity, and selflessness set them above the effete and snobbish aspirants to the world of "Culture." The people I knew were *real* people, not pretenders. They knew precisely what they knew even though they knew nothing of symphonies or ballet or an obscure play by Moliere. But they met and dealt with life, *real* life, and they did so without appearing to be something they were not.

I loved those people for what they were, but I cannot love those who masquerade their way through life professing to be intellectual, when they are not; enlightened, which they will never be; of excellent taste, which if at all, is in their mouths; and cultured, which, because it is such a phony term describing phony people, they just might be.

Day 22.

❈   ❈   ❈

I had some very funny people in my family. An uncle who was continuously funny although he never intended to be, a couple of cousins who loved a good joke, practical or otherwise, and my brother, who was as addicted to humor as I am. He was an avid worshipper of POGO and he got me started. We both think Walt Kelly was king of the hill when it came to comics and philosophy.

One cousin got to be an old guy in his eighties, I think, and he was as funny as an old man as he was when he was younger which I must admit is a difficult thing to be. Old age has a way of making life pretty un-funny most of the time. However, this cousin didn't let his age bother him. Instead he used it as a platform for his jokes. The last time I saw him I asked how he was doing and he replied, "I'm fine as long as they don't run out of body parts." Then, he proceeded to tell me he had had both hips and both knees replaced. Not something I thought of as particularly funny. Then he went on to tell me that both of his knees had broken down on the inside so that they formed an X when he stood up. He also said that he had a friend whose knees had broken down on the outside so that he looked like a O when he was standing and that when both of them stood side-by-side they spelled OX.

He also told me this story of when he was in high school and it's such a good one I don't want to lose it, so I'll put it here in my journal.

When my cousin was in high school there was one kid who suffered from a cleft palate and spoke with a distinct lisp. He also was not the handsomest nor the smartest boy in the class and was generally shunned by the girls. His name was Wilber.

At a school dance Wilber marched over to the prettiest girl in school and asked her for a dance, to which she replied, "Of course not, don't be ridiculous, I'd never dance with you!" Naturally this greatly offended Wilber and he responded somewhat vehemently, saying, "All right then, you can juth kisth my assth!" The girl took umbrage at that and said, "You can't talk to me that way, I'll tell my brother, and he'll beat the hell out of you."

She did indeed talk to her brother who championed her cause, promptly cornered Wilber, and with a threatening fist held in his face, said," You apologize to my sister right now or I will beat the shit out of you."

Wilber reluctantly but necessarily agreed and marched back into the dance hall, sought out the sister, and said to her, "You don't have to kissth my assth, your brother and I have made other arrangethmenths."

Day 23.

"…rainy days and Mondays always get me down."

—Song

❦　　　❦　　　❦

I am dispirited…down in the dumps…ready to throw in the towel…jump down, turn around, and throw the dog a bone…I'm nuts…off my rocker…not playing with a full deck…one brick short of a full load…one can short of a six-pack. In other words, I'm depressed. Charlie and I are both depressed. I can't call on him to be upbeat when I'm so down and out. That's the trouble with having a fantasy friend, he just mirrors the mood you're in. I try to get him up and running but he just sits and sulks. What the hell? Why did I create him if he's not going to help me stay positive?

One thing, it's this damn rain. Sometimes I think I *will* go crazy. That's when I start talking aloud to Charlie, hoping we'll get in an argument, and he'll get me fired up again. Our conversations have been far too serious lately and I think that's what has got me down. We had a long one about God. It's hard to squeeze a little levity out of that conversation. Anyway, I made some notes afterward and this is what we talked about:

It occurred to me during my conversation with Charlie that we live in "Infinity," every moment, every day, all of our lives. Maybe others recognize this; I never did until now. What I mean by infinity is the classic definition of the word "infinite," which is: 1. Extending indefinitely; 2. Immeasurably or inconceivably great or extensive, 3. Subject to no limitation or external determination; 4. Extending beyond, lying beyond, or being greater than any preassigned finite value however large; 5. Characterized by an infinite number of elements or terms. Coincidentally, this happens to be my definition of God.

I wrote a poem once that commented on the infinite variety and shapes of clouds and closed with the line that "all the world beholds infinity." Now, after my current reflections on the subject I believe that the world beholds infinity constantly but that, perhaps, we have never looked at the world that way.

Think of anything around you, grass, trees, people, whatever, and then consider that these things are not duplicates of each other but each is an individual construction. No two blades of grass are identical, no two trees, certainly, no two people (not even so-called "identical" twins). For even as their outward appearance may seem identical, look further, look at their roots and by that I do not mean simply the physical roots that bind them to the earth but the cellular roots, and even atomic make-up of each individual or if that does not satisfy you, look at their mental, emotional, and spiritual makeup. There you will find differences.

Recognizing this gave me a whole new perspective of the things around me. It's a wonderful way to look at the world.

Day 24.

"…but to sing, to laugh, to dream, to walk in my own way,
and be alone, free to see things as they are…"

—Rostand

❧   ❧   ❧

It occurred to me that people talk about miracles, as though a miracle was something stupendous and supernatural. They regard miracles as single events that take place in metaphysical settings and circumstances. This seems to be what everyone thinks of as a miracle. Let there be a little girl hallucinating the image of the Holy Mother of Christ and the whole world goes bonkers.

Good lord, look around, we live in an infinity of miracles. They're all around us everyday. We don't have to go looking for them. The whole world is a bloody miracle.

Look at the conception, gestation and birth of anything, look at the development of the human fetus in the womb, the migration of cells to their assigned positions, the miraculous agglomeration of cells to form eyes, and hands, and organs and all the complex and intricate systems of the human body.

Look at any mammal or ocean organism or bird and find in all of them the miracle of life in all environments, everywhere you look. Look at the microcosm and find there an entire other world of creatures of infinitesimal size but still alive and functioning much like each higher tier of living specie.

Look at all of nature and the connectedness of it all; the symbiosis of plants and animals; the homeostasis of predator and prey; the complex and intricate interdependencies throughout all of mother nature; the cosmic dance of insects and birds and animals and fish and plants of all kinds.

It's all a miracle. All life is a miracle. Much more so than the imagined miracles of religious zealots who can find miracles only in the bizarre.

Day 25.

"…put out my hand and touched the face of God."

—John Gillespie McGee

❦　　　❦　　　❦

I guess I would be categorized as a Deist, as one who sees God in everything. Actually I don't "see God in everything," rather I believe God *is* everything.

Semantically, if you really examine it, the very definition of God encompasses all. We are not separate from a personalized being we call God. God is all pervasive; there is nothing but God. At least that's my belief.

There are as many definitions of God as there are people. Some like God hot and some like God cold. There are those that believe God doesn't exist and those that are so sure that he/she/it does, that they willing to kill themselves (or their children), to be with him/her/it. When it comes to God people are really over the edge. We don't know what the hell we're talking about.

I have stated my belief but in the Judeo-Christian faith God is personified, made to look like a larger man, (thank you Mr. Michelangelo), he occupies a part of the unseen world like a beneficent overlord who looks down on his "children" and either rewards or punishes them according to divine law. In Islamic faith "Allah" assumes much the same position. I find this all rather difficult to understand but then I am a confirmed heretic where Christianity and Islam are concerned. I cannot share many of the beliefs of the either dogma although I subscribe to a great many of their principles and basic precepts.

But to continue, since I believe that everything is God by whatever characteristics God is described, i.e. creator, universal mind, universal spirit, etc., I do believe in God, otherwise, I could not believe in myself.

I love life in all its manifestations. Leo Tolstoy said that, "…he who loves life loves God." I guess I fit that bill.

Day 26.

"Myself when young did eagerly frequent
Doctor and Saint, and heard great argument
About it and about: but evermore
Came out by the same door whence in I went."

—Rubaiyat of Omar Khyyam

❧   ❧   ❧

I have speculated a lot about God, and nature, and people, and I think that we're undoubtedly the worst of God's creatures but then we all have this damnable big brain that causes us to wrestle with life, all of our life. All of us take life and death so seriously. Here I am at 70 and I'm still taking it seriously. When down deep I really believe that it isn't serious at all. How can it be serious if we all die at the end of it and there is nothing but oblivion waiting for us after death?

If anything it's a learning experience, especially if you believe in reincarnation, which I do. And, if it's not that, then it very well may be a cosmic joke, but then there would have to be someone or something that would laugh, wouldn't there? I prefer my first conclusion.

Maybe we are doing precisely what we're supposed to do. Take life seriously, play the game, make the best of the cards we're dealt, and do our best to make our lives meaningful, at least to us. It is not easy to make these types of general observations without thinking that all the religious people on the planet exhibit the same kind of arrogance that I just have in stating unsubstantiated opinions about things we know nothing about.

It is useless to speculate about such things as God and life and death. We do not, indeed, cannot, "know" without qualification the truth of such things. All we can do is persist in bothering the questions and find in all of them the answers that satisfy each individual the most. But, along with our certitude in whatever truth we think we know, be assured that we are, undoubtedly, wrong.

Another poem:

<blockquote>
I have had to learn to wait,
To slow my hurried gait,
To pass slow moments of my time,
And reconcile to a lesser fate.

Time-wearied my life is spent
Quiescent but in torment,
Watching it slowly slip away,
And seeing me inconsequent.

Is this what it has been about?
All my travels to bring me hence,
To where I see my phantom form,
For a time too brief,
Among the scattered stars?

To bring me to the chasm,
At the brink of understanding,
To peek behind the mask of life,
To find that all is change,
That nothing truly matters.

Now I understand,
This then is my destiny.
I was not brought here
To build or create or achieve,
Or leave behind some heritage.
</blockquote>

But simply to live,
To fill my days with living,
To wander through the world,
In awe of all this beauty.

It is enough.

Day 27.

"Where ignorance is bliss,
'Tis folly to be wise."

—Gray

❧   ❧   ❧

Charlie, I've been thinking.

That's always dangerous.

Yeah, but I can't help it. It's a flaw in my character. I wonder if other people indulge in my kind of thinking?

You'll never know.

I know. Here's what I was thinking about. The world's all fucked up. It's upside down. We don't do the things we should and we do the things we shouldn't.

Got any examples?

Yeah, how about giving money to countries who admittedly hate us?

Good one, any more.

Well, I could say the same about us being in countries to protect them against their enemies when they protest us being there. Can't we take a hint?

Score two. Anymore?

Yes. It seems to me that probably we are the most hated people in the world, Americans, I mean, and I think I know why.

Pray tell.

Affluence. When these foreign countries think of us they think of affluence, how rich we all are and how poor the rest of the world is, like themselves, and there's some truth in that. Have the poor ever loved the rich in all of history? I don't think so. There are a lot of poor countries and poor people in the world and, by comparison, we must look like a bunch of rich, arrogant bastards who don't give a damn about the rest of the world. They must think we're only interested in money and I can see where it would seem that way to them. It seems that way to me.

So here they are, many of them starving, or at least on the border, disease ridden, watching their children waste away until they die, and here are the Americans spending a lot of money and research on how to save as many pre-mature babies as possible. That wouldn't be much comfort to a mother say in Eritrea or Ethiopia or Zimbabwe, or Mozambique, or a dozen other countries around the world whose babies lay in their arms sucking on a dry and withered pap.

And, what of this modern penchant for deifying some social celebrity or Rock Star who dies in a traffic accident or in a plane crash while millions of children die each year from malaria and dysentery and dirty water and starvation. What kind of people are we when one life means more than countless others who are suffering far worse deaths than those of the advantaged. Wouldn't you say that's a case of misplaced values?

Yes. Of course.

We spend untold billions on education in this country and have lousy schools where most of the kids don't learn the things that are truly important to make them into the kind of responsible citizens it takes to sustain a democracy, things like morality and ethics and responsibility and, for God's sake, how to manage your finances and stay healthy and how to make intelligent choices, how to incorporate discipline into your life, and the values and rewards of living a good life. How to value the things that we all take for granted like freedom, and liberty (there is a difference you know) and the rights of the individual and the value of family and friends and neighbors. I'm rambling aren't I?

Yes, you are.

Well, it gets to me ever now and then. I look at high school parking lots and see the millions of dollars worth of automobiles sitting there belonging to the students who are inside, not learning a hell of a lot, or wanting to, and it all seems so out of proportion, so unbalanced, so unfair, to have half the world with not enough and a parking lot full of the cars of teenagers. The world's fucked up. You see what I mean?

Yes, It's pretty obvious in those and many more examples. It is all fucked up. Is there one word to describe this fucked-upped-ness?

Yeah…it's called, "Civilization."

Day 28.

"There is a place I know,
Far, far away,
Where you get beans to eat,
Three times a day…"

—Old Soldier's song

❦　　　❦　　　❦

Well, I'm back among the living, having shed my depression of the last week or so. I'm determined not to get mired down in self-pity or in mindless, endless diatribes with Charlie. Life's too short to spend energy on these meanderings through the world of the metaphysical or the physical for that matter.

However, weighty questions are the only ones worth considering. It may be entertaining to talk about humor or horses or bumper stickers but for the seriously minded there are better things to do with one's mind.

Charlie and I were considering World War Two and the Nazis and the killing of fifty million people and why people do such things? What is it in man that makes us so good at killing one another and so bad at perpetuating peace? Those are questions one can get his teeth into.

I have read a great deal about the Third Reich and the Nazis, trying valiantly to understand how the rise of Hitler and the virtual enslavement of a country of 80 million people could have happened. How could people not have sensed the evil personified in the character of Hitler and the Nazis? Further, I have wondered if it was a happening peculiar to the Germans or could something similar and as bad happen to other people?

First of all, what Hitler and the Nazis did is unusual in the history of man-kind only because of the scale of the atrocity not because it was singularly unique. A cursory study of history clearly illustrates that mankind has killed as wantonly, espoused genocide, and perpetuated crimes equally evil against other peoples as anything the Germans did. In fact we have witnessed con-certed efforts at genocide only recently in Africa (the Hutus and the Tutsis) and in Yugoslavia (the Serbs out to kill off the Muslim Bosnians). Or, review our own history and evaluate some of our actions regarding the Native Ameri-cans. Go back further to the Crusades and the Inquisition and the Golden Horde of Genghis Khan and to Alexander the Great and to the biblical geno-cide of the Philistines by the Jews. Read on and on about how good we are at exterminating each other.

But what made the German nation opt to become the world's premiere bad guy of all time? Of course what we now call Germans at one time were many tribes of "barbarians" that even the Roman Empire could not subdue, so they may come by their aggressive nature genetically. Be that as it may, the nation, as we now recognize it, did not begin to emerge until the mid-1800's. It was Prussia, Bohemia, Austria, Hungary, the Palatinate, and various small king-doms each governed by kings under the aegis of the remnants of the Holy Roman Empire.

When Kaiser Wilhelm the First fought and conquered France in the war of 1870 he began the building of the Germany that shows up on our maps today. That's only slightly over a hundred years ago. That successful war served to assuage the rude handling of all of these countries at the hand of Napoleon I, bolster the warlike attitudes of the Prussian military, and, of course, embitter the French to the point where they ousted the second empire (under Napoleon the third) and re-instated the republic.

This Prussian victory paved the way for the consolidation of the nations of central Europe into one entity—Germany, and that way led inevitably to World War I.

Day 29.

❦   ❦   ❦

Boy, I'm getting preachy; I really hate that in me. I get on a kick, talking about things I probably shouldn't, and I go a little nuts. It's a flaw in my character. But then I said I was going to use this time to write whatever in the hell I wanted. So if I do carry on a bit too much what difference does it make?

It's just that it's a sign that I really do take life seriously and I believe that's a big mistake. A person should closely watch themselves in regard to philosophy or deep thoughts, either will eventually confuse you, or estrange your family and friends. About as deep as a person should go in analyzing life or oneself or for that matter, much of anything else, is about the depth of a gnat's ass. This will not be very satisfying intellectually but it will keep you out of trouble. Come to think of it (oh, boy, there I go again) this seems to be about the level of thought enjoyed by most people. But then intellectual thought or the slightest bit of self-examination is guaranteed to give you a headache.

It is this kind of statement that is certain to draw dirty looks from my wife along with a somewhat disgusted explative to the effect that I am an intellectual snob with absolutely no right to be. She's probably correct.

Speaking of my wife, I remembered a conversation we had many times over the years we've been together, it is this, that along with great love lies great responsibility. Both she and I recognize this responsibility. Simply put it is that we so love each other that whatever one of us would sincerely want to do the other would not only concede to but gladly go along. If for example I said I wanted to move to New England; that it was vitally important to me; she would say, "Okay, let's go."

Now that's where the responsibility comes in. Because each of us knows that if something is that important to either of us then the other one would readily agree and that puts the person wanting that important thing whatever it is, in a position where you better be damn sure that you want it bad enough to upset your life over it. It is this responsibility that keeps me from acting like a selfish ass and deciding that I'm tired of a certain routine and want to do something dramatic like move to New England. It makes me consider her and her wishes and her circumstances. Therefore, I try not to demand anything that would put me in the category of an insensitive dolt and mess up our lives with selfish demands. I know I could be a selfish idiot and she would support me in doing whatever I wanted but that knowledge keeps me from doing it. That responsibility derives from something I call—love.

Day 30.

❦   ❦   ❦

If you wish to create an embittered enemy, study the Versailles treaty which was forced on the German nation after the First World War. Make your enemy crawl beneath your demands for his land, his money, his abject humiliation, and his future. Make your demands for restitution such that you condemn his entire nation to poverty, run-away inflation, unemployment, and industrial collapse. Then you can be assured that sooner or later he will rise with fatal determination to revenge the damage you have caused and to visit that damage and more upon you.

This was the heritage for the Germans after WW I and the treaty of Versailles. The emergence of the Third Reich could not have happened if the French had not been so intent upon the punishment imposed in the treaty.

Every German felt the humiliation in the loss of the war. They were a proud people. And, the financial straits that the nation suffered was tantamount to ensuring that they would never be powerful enough to again stand among the mighty nations of the world.

Even though their lives had been turned upside down by the war and its aftermath, one wonders how all of the German people could subscribe to the insanity of the Third Reich. Well let us think for a moment. When Hitler first came to power he was doing great things for the country. Chief among which was putting people back to work but also restoring the infrastructure of the country with new building, new roads, new railroads, and covertly rebuilding the military power of the country. All most Germans saw of the evil side of the Hitler regime was the strutting SA and SS troops who paraded through the streets and in the arenas of the largest cities. Very few knew of the political intrigues and manipulations that characterized Hitler's rise to power. When a person is on the inside of a culture it is difficult to see or understand the movement of that culture. It is like being on the inside of a circle where one only sees that segment of the circle on which he focuses, only if one is outside the circle does the whole circle become apparent.

So my theory is that while things were improving and the economy was getting better and the despair was lifting from the miasma that previously shrouded the country, it is no wonder that people endured the rise of what most of them might have eschewed in other times. I analogize it to a flowing river with a crowd of people standing on the river banks and because of the smooth flow and the inviting pleasure of the water the crowd moves slowly into the shallows and because the river's pull is insistent they move into deeper water little by little until the river catches them and they are pulled along into the current where they no longer are capable of escaping. Given the circumstances within Germany at the time, I believe any people would have reacted similarly.

Day 31.

"…I'm Bewitched, I'm Bothered, I'm Bemildred."

—Walt Kelly—POGO

❧   ❧   ❧

Charlie did I ever tell you about my wanting wavy hair?

No, of course not, but I know the story.

Of course you do. Well, when I was a kid I had a head full of dark straight hair that came too far down on my forehead. Straight across. No widow's peak, no arching back at the sides, just straight across. It was awful. And, I got to thinking about how it would look at least a little better if I had just one wave in front, so I could comb it to one side or the other and accentuate the wave.

Therefore, you gave yourself a permanent.

No. I put a strong rubber band over my head where I wanted the wave to be and pulled it down under my chin about half way up my jaw, then I went to bed thinking I would have this wonderful wave in the morning.

You were a boy genius.

I woke up in the middle of the night and my entire face was dead. The rubber band had cut off all circulation to my face and it had no feeling whatever. I jumped out of bed, went into the bathroom and looked in the mirror. My face was dead white. I quickly removed the rubber band and rubbed my face to get some circulation back into it. And, then I saw it. The most beautiful wave you have ever seen arching across the front of my hair just short of the hairline. It was gorgeous and I took several minutes primping my hair while my face was busy reconstituting itself.

I had succeeded. I now had a wave in my hair that would be the envy of every guy and girl in school. I was overjoyed thinking I wouldn't look like a schmuck any longer but someone with character, with suaveness, with a wave.

I went back to bed thinking of what an impression I would make upon the morrow's morn and off to pleasant dreams I went. When I arose in the morning I went immediately to the bathroom and looked intently into the mirror. The wave was gone. My face had returned to normal but so had my damnable hair.

About a year later my hair suddenly started getting wavy. At first it was just the back of my head but over several months it moved progressively forward until my entire head was covered with undulating waves of hair. So wavy in fact that I began disliking the unruliness of all these waves that I could never keep in long rolling undulations but rather insisted on progressing into tight curls.

So, I would whack them off and get my hair under control for about a week before my rebel curls would come back and begin to stick out in all directions like an aberrant cactus. It wasn't a pretty sight, and I began to hate waves and especially curls. I got crew cuts and Butch cuts and each time it came back worse than before. I would plaster them down with water before I went out on dates but during the evening they would dry out and spring forth with a determination that could only be likened to an angry, striking Cobra.

I despaired, kept my hair cut as short as possible until I blessedly started going bald. But the back of my head which, to this day has a goodly amount of hair, is still at odds with me. It still waves and curls and would take me over, at least that part of me, it I ever let it get away from my at home, do-it-yourself clippers. I have chopped at it now for 60 years and it still will not give up.

I somehow blame it all on that damn rubber band and my wishing so hard to get a wave in my hair. I think it was all that fervent wanting and hoping and wishing that somehow triggered my hair follicles into doing what they did. Vanity, vanity, all is vanity. If I had known what that damn rubber band would start I would have shot it at one of my friends, let them get a bright idea for its use, and let *them* take the consequences.

Brilliant!

Day 32.

"Stiffen the sinews; summon up the blood…"

—Shakespeare

❦ ❦ ❦

I recently read a book entitled, *My Loyalty Is My Honor*. It was a book of interviews with former SS soldiers, most of whom had been in the Hitler Youth Corps. They told of their indoctrination into Nazism, their schooling, their status and prestige at being the "chosen," to restore the "Fatherland" to its once proud glory. And, guess what? I saw myself and my friends undergoing the same indoctrination and following the same honor and glory that those boys did. We would have relished the thought that we were assigned an important job in the re-creation of our nation. We would have been as good Nazis as any of them.

The Americans have never been challenged as the Europeans have nor have we the bitter hatreds born from the innumerable wars that have ravaged Europe for thousands of years. I venture to say that if we Americans were placed in the same position as were the Germans before WW II we would have been equally as nationalistic, as aggressive, and as brutal as they.

We have proved ourselves to be as destructive of life and property in those sad and lamentable pages of our history when dealing with our American Indians and in our own civil war. In view of these terrible periods in our own history how can we set ourselves up to judge what another people does in the name of nationalism. Is "Manifest Destiny" more justification than any other nationalistic creed? I think not.

Other examples of the American penchant for killing is manifest in our non-discretionary bombing of German and Japanese cities in WWII where hundreds of thousands of civilians were killed, maimed, and otherwise brutalized by our particular version of "total war". The bombing of Dresden, Essen, Berlin, and, in Japan, of Tokyo and, of course, Hiroshima and Nagasaki, attests to our willingness to shed blood. Vietnam is another equally terrible example. So are we so pure? What is it in human nature that makes us so willing to kill members of our own species?

Still another poem:

Somewhere has born a cold wind.
Feel it now?
It chills the heart,
And stills the children's laughter.

It breathes a bitter breath,
Well hidden in the air of freedom,
Disguised in subtle sophistry,
To lead astray the easy,
Cajole and betray the most astute.

It feeds the fear in all men's hearts,
And with its whispering insistence,
Turns out the fear to consume the reason,
And place the angry weapon in the hand.

It is such stuff as makes up war,
When passion has usurped
The place of reason.

Day 33.

"S'wonderful, s'marvelous, that you could care for me…"

—Song—"S'wonderful"

❧   ❧   ❧

I'm worn out. My wife has been back bull-horning me again. She's getting more adamant about my coming down every time she visits. She doesn't know all of the story about why I'm up here, in the rain, hiding behind my drapes, and typing relentlessly on my laptop.

What she doesn't know is that when I announced my intentions of tree sitting for 100 days, three of my dubious friends bet me $1000 that I could not stay the course. In my arrogance I took the bet. Oh, how I wish that I would have backed down, but now I'm in the soup. I can't confess to my wife that I'm coming down, although we will be $1000 lighter in our bank account when I do. Besides it's not the manly thing to do. As if I gave a big rat's ass what the "manly thing to do" is. No, it's more that I would let myself down if I admitted defeat and swung miserably in the basket on the pulley system down to good old terra firma. I can't do that; my unbridled pride won't allow it. Besides there's only 67 more days to go. *Oh God*! I wish I hadn't counted them!

I feel bad not telling my wife about the bet. That is not correct matrimonial behavior and I dearly love my wife. I just figured she'd be better off not knowing. Now I have to live with myself for deceiving her. I'm a real shit.

Why is it that the damn thousand dollars sticks in my craw so much? I'm not money oriented, at least not inordinately so. Money has always played a big part in my life but I've never let it dictate my jobs, my love life, my social relations, or much of anything else. I've recognized its necessity and I've always loved going first class but by and large throughout my life I've spent it as fast as I got it. I enjoyed money; I didn't obsess over it.

That reminds me of a song my Dad used to sing. It was called "The Balled of Sam Bass," and there was one line in it that always kind of reminded me of me. It went like this: "…Sam rode the Denton mare, he matched her at scrub races, and he took her to the fair. Young Sam he coined the money, but he spent it rather free, for he always drank good whiskey, wherever he would be."

Day 34.

"With them the seed of Wisdom did I sow,
And with mine own hand wrought to make it grow;
And this was all the Harvest that I reap'd—
"I came like Water, and like Wind I go."

—Rubaiyat of Omar Khayyam

❧   ❧   ❧

Charlie and I continue our conversations albeit at a much more relaxed pace. We hit on the subject of belief the other day and that gave me some food for thought. Rightly or wrongly this is what I determined:

In a general way I believe in a type of predestination. First of all I became convinced that in very specific terms we are prisoners of our genetics, our race, our parents, schools, religion, and our experiences, especially those of our childhood. All of these things predispose us along one path or another and, depending on our intellectual prowess, we pursue that path relentlessly and generally without question.

Then it occurred to me that there is only one exception to this predisposition inherited or incurred by our genetics or our individual environmental upbringing and that was in the area of our beliefs where we can choose what to believe and in so doing break free of the beliefs that had been impressed in us by our parents, teachers, priests, ministers, and all of the others influencing our lives from the time of birth.

But there is a catch in this "breaking free" for in so doing we establish from the instant of our re-birth a new or, at least different, set of beliefs and, voila', we become the prisoner of those beliefs, only this time by choice. So have we truly liberated ourselves or have we simply rejected one set of rules for another?

Throughout life I think we struggle trying to understand why we are here, and there are a world of religions, sects, cults, and faiths that attempt to define a rationale to answer these questions. Unfortunately, in this attempt to convert the indefinable into rational articulation we must rely on terms not only accommodated by our language but which can convey an understandable concept within the context of our collective reality.

For example, define God. Regardless of how you personally define God your definition becomes part of the belief system you have constructed for yourself and influences (if not controls) the aspects of conscience, morality, ethics, and behavior that you manifest as you proceed through life. If you choose to believe there is no God that belief leads inevitably to another system of behavior. So again you are the prisoner of your beliefs. The fact that you chose these particular beliefs does not alter the fact that you have confined yourself within a religious or philosophical milieu of beliefs that restrict and govern your life.

Now that I am old and have come to the realization that I cannot assimilate all of history nor all of philosophy in one lifetime, let alone comprehend and understand it all, I have arrived at the conclusion that no beliefs may be preferable to any and all that have been manufactured by man. To take the best of every religion, or philosophy, and to have surveyed as much of history as is possible in the short time allowed, and to conscientiously avoid systematizing these random fragments into a new and rational doctrine, may be the best course to follow. It certainly allows the most freedom, and may ultimately provide the best answer to the search for answers to questions that have no answer.

Oh, good heavens, another poem!

Behold the dry cocoons,
Where in silence dwells
The atrophying minds
Of the dying ones.

Self-made cocoons,
Of thought-silk,
Of belief-skin,
And tiny modules

Of memories,
And hopes,
And fears,
All tightly bound,
Confining growth,
Enclosing self,
Denying life.

Depressing, huh?

Day 35.

"Difficulty is a severe instructor…"

—Burke

❦   ❦   ❦

The days flow by and I do mean flow, in a current of rainwater to which there is no end. I am water logged; I am hydrated to the point of ultimate fluidity, threatening to just melt into a pool of liquid protoplasm. I am constantly damp and cold; my joints ache from the dampness; my soul withers, weighted down by too much loneliness and water. A man wasn't intended to live like this. But, when this self-pitying thought occurs to me I have to respond, "Look in the mirror, shithead, you did it to yourself."

And, oh my, I am lonely. I wanted so badly to get away from everyone and everything, and now I'm almost ready to yield to my need for human companionship, descend from my airy perch, pay my pound of flesh to my erstwhile friends, apologize to my wife, daughter and son-in-law, and eat a large helping of crow in front of everyone howling for my downfall. At least I wouldn't be alone.

I am so sick and tired of myself. I am boring, and egocentric, and arrogant in thinking I know a lot more than I do. When you come right down to it, I'm not sure I know anything at all.

I have been doubting my thinking lately. I see it as a form of perverse entertainment, examining everything as though I could define answers to universal questions that have defied the finest minds over many millennia. That, my friends, is real, highest quality, conceit. But what else can I do. I'm all I have. Just me and Charlie. I keep coming back to the fact that my whole world consists of what's in my brain, and frankly, I'm beginning to think that some of my wiring got screwed up somewhere along the way. Indeed, I would like to give it all up. I'm tired of fighting, I just can't find the place you go to surrender.

My thinking comes in fragments now. I find it difficult to hang onto a thought for very long before another enters and crowds out the former one. I may be losing my mind. No. Not really. It's just this deprivation I've sentenced myself to so completely. Sometimes I really dislike me for what I have done to myself. Does that make sense? Am I losing it? Is this the beginning of Alzheimer's disease?

What if material existence is an experiment by God? Following my philosophy of "God is everything" then God chose to devolve into material being in all things material to experience being in materiality. And, because the "Divine Oneness" is all things on all levels of existence the sum of all thoughts and feelings in every action of animate and inanimate material is experienced by God. But there must be levels of existence other than material existence for God, therefore, this must be only one of an infinite number, all experienced by God simultaneously. God must be very busy.

I think I'm losing it.

Day 36.

❈ ❈ ❈

Random Thoughts

A person's life can be analogized to a subatomic particle that can never be seen itself, only where it has been. The streak of light it leaves behind is all we know of it.

❈ ❈ ❈

<u>Meaning equals Experience</u>
<u>Experience equals Meaning</u>

In this expression all lives have meaning. There is no such thing as a wasted life.

❈ ❈ ❈

We are born alone and we die alone. All of our lives we fear aloneness. But if we see our aloneness as just another facet of our lives, with no more importance than any other aspect, and see it also as a significant contributor to our total experience, then it has meaning as great as any of our other experiences, and it becomes a part of our whole being.

❧   ❧   ❧

Living by formula is to obviate choice. Freedom to choose is the most dangerous ground for humans; we are too prone to error and temptation and impulse. The formula of poverty and religion is better than that of poverty and freedom.

❧   ❧   ❧

Man is more deserving of our compassion than any other being for, because of our big brains, we are burdened far more than any other creature. Animals are led by instinct but we direct our lives based on learned behavior, a ritual of beliefs, myths, concepts, ideas, all distorted by our personal egotism; our vague perception of the world around us; the total evolution of the race of man that has preceded us; the words, the art, the music, the milieu of our time; and the constructs of our individual reality. We are the least to be admired and the most to be pitied.

❧   ❧   ❧

Among the games we play,
Is the Poet's, Odd-Man-Out.

It is destiny
That drives the world,
Not ideals.
Economics rules over us,
And romance only finds
A place in lover's arms,
In darkened rooms,

And unturned pages
In dusty books.

Science turns
The human part of us,
Into atoms,
That group and gather
In peculiar forms,
That makes us go
Mechanically,
Without choice.

My soul darkens
At these thoughts,
And strives for air
Above these cruel images,
To seek release
In tree-grown mountain sides,
And clouds and sky,
And the out-stretched freedom
Of the wild geese.

Day 37.

"In her starry shade
Of dim and solitary loveliness,
I learn the language of another world."

—Byron

❧　　　❧　　　❧

Looked at through the Mind's Eye, we live in a "Divine Soup," but we are ill-equipped except in our imagination to perceive it so. By "Divine Soup" I mean on an atomic level, and if our eyesight was at the intensity of an electron microscope we would see nothing but a giant admixture of atoms swirling about in gravity-controlled space.

If our sight and other senses were at that enhanced degree we would be able to see the infinity of forms materializing and de-materializing from this amalgam of atoms. And we would be struck by the sameness and inter-connectedness of it all; that we ourselves are nothing more than part of that soup; and that "soup" is the first tangible part of God behind which is only "will"; the will to life, the will to be, the will to create, the will to beauty, the will to joy.

We humans do not like such metaphysical wanderings. Rather we want continuity, the hard firmament under our feet; knowing that the sun will arise each morning; that trees and grass and flowers will bloom in the Spring; in short, that all the days will follow a logical and contiguous pattern, at least, to our eyes.

We enjoy history as a confirmation of our present and our future, but if we can entertain both our physical awareness and perhaps a higher one (that of a

"Divine Soup"?), we can perhaps begin to perceive ourselves differently, a little more integrated with life, a little more compassionate, understanding, and joyful, and even, perhaps, see ourselves as part of the infinite.

As if by a dream enlightened,
I see myself in this brief day of life,
Surreal in its course and brevity.
In inexorable motion,
In indeterminate direction,
Adrift in high bright seas,
Loose among the cluttered heavens.

As if in a dream enlightened,
I view the tumultuous throng
Which surrounds my small perception.
Sojourners all,
In continuum,
On a river of time.

As if in a dream enlightened,
I see the torrent of faces,
Reflecting lives within lives,
Within and around each other,
And my own.

As if in a dream enlightened,
I hear the soft sweet music
Of the movement of the Earth,
The harmony of life,
Punctuated by the hush
Of the eternal.

Day 38.

"It little profits that an idle king,
By this still hearth…"

—Tennyson

❦   ❦   ❦

It occurred to me that all I can do is look backward. I can't see the future, so all I have is my past and what little I have learned from it. Oh, I speculate, as one can see from my previous writings, but that's all it is, speculation. What impressed me about this was the fact that everything I brought with me in my head was in the past. The present which is me sitting in a clamshell trying not to get wet, means little if anything.

Everything I know is behind me. That's my only resource. As a result I use my memory extensively and I think it is pretty accurate although I think one tends to romanticize the past somewhat. I know I do when thinking of my boyhood. It probably was never as good as I remember it to be. But, we all have to accept what we are and that includes what we think and what we remember.

If you come right down to it, our past is all we bring with us no matter where we go; what we are, meaning our character, our morals, ethics, beliefs, etc.; what we think in terms of our reaction to the environment at the moment; and what we remember. That's all there is to us. We can't look forward; we have no visibility of the future; we can hypothesize but we don't do that very well, things change too fast. And, if we could predict the future with any accuracy, life wouldn't be as challenging, varied, colorful, poignant, or fulfilling. That would take the fun out of it.

A poem based on this deduction:

>Something in man turns ever back,
>From the all-absorbing moment,
>To some lost beck'ning day
>Not quite remembered
>Not yet forgot.
>
>We stand too close to time,
>And the moment has no character.
>Like all things, time must be caressed
>By memories and shaped
>Through use and purpose
>To have meaning.
>
>Meaning is lost in the *Now*.
>We walk from Yesterday,
>Into the future,
>From known,
>To unknown,
>And see nothing now
>Except disjointed time,
>A meaningless moment
>Without shape, without color,
>And with no hope of reason,
>Until it too lies at our back.
>
>But turn us round again,
>To see those older days,
>Well-ordered and in context,
>A lifetime set in history.
>
>There we find the time that's lost,
>But never was–
>Till now.

Day 39.

"...there the Wiffenpoofs assemble..."

—Song—Yale University

❧   ❧   ❧

Today is only partially cloudy so I can open my cage and get some air flowing around me. It is chilly, but warm enough, about 60 degrees, I'd guess.

I've lost track of the days. I don't know what day it is. Not that it matters. I don't have anything to do today that is any different than any other day. It's just that somehow knowing what day it is gives some concreteness to your life. You think, Oh, boy! It's Saturday, I'll have some entertainment of some kind today. Or, today's Sunday, I'll take the whole day off, no work of any kind, I'll just declare a holiday. Or, okay, it's Monday, time to get started with something, pay bills, take the car in for an oil change, do the shopping I put off Friday. See what I mean? Concreteness. You think you know where you are in time. And that knowledge is a great comfort. I know, I've lost it. Next time my wife bullhorns me I'll ask her what day it is. Except then she really will think I've lost it.

Charlie and I have been having a conversation about family trees. My tree supposedly extends back to a Norman forebear who helped the Duke of Normandy invade England in 1066. There's a little gap of 700 years or so where no one kept track of our lineage. But according to a small book called, *Memoirs of a Nonagenarian,* the first of my American branch came from England in 1721 to Charleston, South Carolina. He married a local girl, whose father was very wealthy, and started his own dynasty.

Of the children of that marriage, some stayed in Charleston, at least one moved to Virginia, then he or another moved to Kentucky, then he or one of his sons moved to Iowa. That's where my great grandfather is buried. I've been to his grave. My grandfather left Iowa to go to Colorado, then Oklahoma, then back to Colorado. That's the long and the short of it.

It's all very interesting but of what good is that knowledge? We all die and unless you believe in reincarnation, and believe that you'll be reincarnated into the same family, all that nonsense doesn't mean squat. At this point I don't know what I believe, and reincarnation is a distant possibility anyway. It may or may not be. No one can answer that.

Examining the travels of my forebears, I wonder what all that striving, that wandering, that impulse to push further and further West, that determined pioneering was about. Was it an attempt just to improve their economic circumstances, or was it the desire for adventure to see new country, to challenge the elements and the land, or to fulfill a destiny that they did not consciously recognize but only felt deep within themselves.

I suspect that the lust for adventure did indeed influence my grandfathers as it did their fathers before them but I don't believe any such desire filled the bosoms of my grandmothers. Theirs was the hardest task and the lot of a pioneering wife was anything but gentle. So what was it that drove all those people to do what they did?

Looking back on them from my perspective I see all the romance and adventure and wonderful freedom and joy in their wanderings but I know it was not that way. It was hard and severe, and full of sweat and pain, and never ending toil. It was a test of every nerve and sinew, and of one's beliefs and determination and persistence and stamina. It was a challenge to all of nature by minuscule animals who, emboldened by God knows what, chose to place themselves in jeopardy in the great expanse of the West; the roaring winds; the harsh and killing winters; the ever-changing and fickle weather; the desolation and aloneness in a land that had no succor, not close friends, nor doctors, nor running water, nor power of any kind save that of horses or mules or one's own back; where children were indeed a blessing because they could work along with you and try, as you tried, to make the land habitable and the least bit congenial.

Day 40.

"…for time and chance happeneth to us all…"

—Ecclesiastes

❦   ❦   ❦

Again thinking of my forebears I tried to envision what their lives might have been that would have called upon them to move into that vastness, that void, called the West, about which very little was known. To make that attempt in wooden wagons that creaked and bounced and swayed across the open prairies into and out of ravines and gorges and rivers and valleys and over mountains, up the steep sides and down the precarious faces of those mountains to get to a place where, by some mysterious reckoning they assumed they had come to make it theirs.

Would I have done the same thing, or would I have been content to stay with others of my kind in the established towns and cities with their marginal civilization and pretenses at society and sophistication and culture? In all probability I would have gone for even now I do not much like the so-called civilized world that I find myself a part of, and remembering when I was a young man, I loved the challenge of jumping into the unknown; of taking a risk; of long, hard winters; of testing and trying my abilities and my strength; and exulting simply in the joy of living.

Was their intent, perhaps, in Thoreau's words "….because I wished to live deliberately, to front only the essential facts of life, and see if I could not learn what it had to teach, and not, when I came to die, discover that I had not lived."

I should have liked to go along with my grandfather on his wanderings; been a part of his adventure; shared the freedom and the excitement of the frontier; seen more of nature and been more a part of it. By comparison my life is pale and deprived of the substance which made his life seem so vital and dynamic and mine so concocted and one-dimensional. However, it is always easy to look backward and say I should have liked to have done that.

But time and circumstances cast us in a mold from the day we are born and you have to play the cards you're dealt, like it or not.

So my point is, that if you can trace your ancestry back to the first caveman to move from the cave to the savanna, what difference does it make? Does that, in any way improve your present existence? I guess it might give you some roots, and if it does, and that makes you happy, then a person ought to do it. But, I'm not sure that continuity is real. Who can say with any certainty that he is the progeny of all those people that preceded him. And, even if he says it. What difference does it make?

There was a time when learning about my ancestry gave me a sense of being anchored to the earth and it was a good thing. I've since become old, and jaded, and too dubious of almost everything to enjoy it anymore.

That was the essence of Charlie's and my conversation and as you can see it led us nowhere except into the arena of the metaphysical where there are only questions, without answers. That sort of thing is just more mental masturbation that, much like its physical counterpart, leaves you somewhat satisfied, but always...alone.

Where does mind and spirit
Commingle to become the one?
Am I all earth,
Only witnessed by my real self,
Learning, by experiencing the world,
To return to ether,
To cogitate the journey?

Then why this sadness now,
That surfaces in the reflection
Of lost days
And threatened futures?

Day 41.

"Liebestod"

—Wagner

❀　　　❀　　　❀

Music has to be the finest accomplishment of man. It certainly is the one thing in the world of art that lives longest, with the possible exception of some Greek and Roman architecture, and the many paintings that have long lives, by de Vinci, Michelangelo, and many others who deserve serious praise. But you don't see a de Vinci or a Michelangelo, a Degas, Goya, Monet, van Gogh, or a Cézanne, etc. every day, however, you can hear the great music of Mozart, Tchaikovsky, Mendelssohn, Rimsky-Korsakov, Borodin, Wagner, Rachmaninoff, and on and on, as often as you like, through the simple medium of radio or a CD player. See? I'm not entirely anti-technology.

If you're lucky you might also hear some of the great old love songs and jazz from the forties and fifties or even some of the folk music from the sixties and seventies. There was some good modern music at one time or another.

I don't know what happened to music. Except for the music coming from some Broadway shows, all I hear is trash. I don't even understand the words and if I do, I wish I hadn't. Maybe it's just a phase present generations are going through. I sure hope so.

I hope the same thing about literature. I haven't read any since Sholokhov's *Quiet Flows The Don.* I expect there have been some worthy books written that I have missed but I haven't heard of any. I'm talking about *great* literature, Sholokhov's work is definitely in that category but I've read a dozen or more

Pulitzer Prize winners since Sholokhov won the prize, and I wouldn't classify any of them as "great."

But then I'm very cynical about our current society. I don't see much of significance or substance in it. As a country we've certainly grown in numbers of people and money and power but in terms of the arts we're down the tubes. I think we once were a great people in the areas of literature, poetry, art, and music but somewhere along the way we entered the wasteland, and at least a great many of our the young seem to be content to dwell in it. They listen to ear-rupturing Rap and Rock, while pulsating stroboscopic lights sweep across their gyrating bodies in an orgy of sounds and sights and wildness induced by the biggest misnomer of them all, "Ecstasy." God, how much further down must we go?

I know I'm probably wrong in my castigation of the young. God knows I was no exalted example of morality when I was a young man. All I can say in my defense was that I read classic books, listened both to classical music and modern jazz, took a college course in art appreciation so that I'd have some idea of what constituted good from awful, and tried valiantly to write poetry that was, if not good at least acceptable.

That doesn't excuse my excoriation of the several generations that came on line in the 1960s and have since gone (in my estimation) from questionable to extreme. I suppose my parents thought my generation was aberrant according to their times and their upbringing. Maybe every generation feels the same. It's just that I feel so alien anymore when I find myself in the company of young people. They probably feel the same way. Isn't human nature strange?

Of course, we live in a truly different world now. For hundreds of years before the world became an urban world I think there was less of a generational gap. When we were a rural people we lived in natural time in tune with the seasons and with the prior and subsequent generations. Now that we are urbanized and computerized, nothing remains constant for very long. Now the level of our patience is about as long as it takes for our computer to boot up. And with that acceleration of time we have so excited our nervous systems that we are less tolerant, less caring, less loving, and perhaps, less willing to admit our own inadequacies and more willing to lay the blame for the condition of the world on newer generations. If that's what I'm doing, I beg your pardon.

Day 42.

"Thirty days hath September, April, June, and November,
All the rest have thirty-one except Gramma who has false teeth."

—Anon

❧   ❧   ❧

I still do not know what day it is, I think it's Tuesday but I'm just guessing. It's just a day like all of them have been since I was roped up here, to sit, usually in the half light of a rainy day, and talk to myself, (sorry Charlie), and write down idiotic words in a diary.

It would be a different story if I were on safari in Africa. But to sit up here in my obscure aerie, day after miserable day, with nothing going on except what is in my head, is the height of stupidity. I must have been insane to do this thing, although I will say that it has given me some new insights that I probably would never have discovered had I continued to lead a normal life.

Normal? What the hell is a "Normal" life? I imagine that what most people regard as normal is the heretofore typical: get born; go to grade school; go to high school; go to college; get married; get a job; beget children; buy a house; buy all the things that make one comfortable, cars, furniture, gadgets, toys; go to work everyday; save for retirement; retire; wonder what it was all about; and die. Normal? Whew! I hope not.

I couldn't help but write a poem about this.

I am not fitted to a comfortable life,
For therein a restlessness is born,
Which destroys all about me
In vain attempt to achieve
Those circumstances
Which prepossess my nature.

To find life
In all its eloquence,
Its trial, its fervor, its passion.

I cannot live by being dead.

Life the challenge, consumes me,
And to find a few but wonderful
Moments of it
Would be worth a hundred years
Of mediocrity.

Day 43.

❦   ❦   ❦

I spent some time thinking about my childhood, my adulthood, and my retirement. It all seems to have gone so fast. Somebody speeded up the camera. Anyway, after musing over my past at some length, I remembered the statement that Dizzy Dean made when he retired from baseball. When he announced his retirement to a group of reporters, one of them asked, "What's the trouble Diz? The old arm give out on you?" to which Diz replied, "Well, it's not as good as it used to be, but then what the hell is?" A very appropriate statement for the way I feel about things nowadays. And, I think sooner or later everyone will say the same thing.

There truly is, believe it or not, a generation gap. My generation is so different from the present one that it is hard to believe we are of the same specie. I don't relate to kids anymore, especially teenagers, but then does anybody really relate to teenagers, except, maybe, other teenagers?

I wasn't exactly understandable as a teen, I had a lot of growing-up problems. My mother always referred to my teenage-hood as "going over fool's hill." Very appropriate, I'd say.

With all of this in mind, I wrote another poem:

Time again has changed his masque
And with it turned my eyes
Toward death
And left the taste of dust
Upon my mouth.
Brief moment fly,
Ere these unspoken doubts
And nameless fears
Sweep aside my faint and halting trust,
And see me wrecked,
And wretched in despair.

Not long ago the world
Seemed a new exciting place,
Somewhere outside my valley,
Beyond the all-surrounding mountains,
Beyond the quiet fields
And orchards that kept
The pheasants and the quail,
And hid the meadowlark from view.
Beyond the river,
And the dry, washed earth
Above the waters edge,
Beyond the pale
And little life
Of small-town childhood.

Somewhere out there,
I viewed the world
Through child's eyes,
And some divine insight
Into what ought to be.

But time betrays the children,
Revealing dreams as dreams,
Distorting wishes into stern reality,
Requiring not so much ideal,
As courage to endure.

Day 44.

"It was the best of times, it was the worst of times."

—Dickens

❈   ❈   ❈

I think my father and mother were the most courageous people I've ever known. Unlike bravery, courage is far more subtle and is expressed differently. I see bravery as diving into a raging river to pull someone out of the rushing water, or running into a blazing house-fire to rescue a child, or charging into machine gun fire to defeat an enemy. That's bravery and bravery is a component of courage for certainly all brave actions require courage. But there is a quiet courage that is seldom noticed and never celebrated. That is what my parents had.

With only a sixth grade education my father had to brave the world, make a living and support his family. He carried a lot on his shoulders. Ten or more years of his struggle to make a living were during the Great Depression of the 1930s, where I know he was out of work most of the time. And, when he could find work it was usually at the rate of a dollar a day. His courage bespoke itself in the very fact that he endured everyday and strived to give his family food, clothing, a roof over our heads, and as many comforts as our pitiful financial condition would allow.

My father worked at many things but mostly he was a house painter and during the Depression he traded a lot of his labor for things such as dentistry, doctors, and eyeglasses. He worked for a time for my uncle who owned and operated a truck line, and for the Public Service Company on the Gas Gang.

He also worked for the railroad, painting signs of all sorts concerned with safety in the railroad yard and at crossings all across the state.

I never heard him complain about the work he did or the lack of work that kept us so poor. He took whatever came along without so much as a whimper and did the best he could under the prevailing circumstances. He was a courageous man for taking the responsibility he assumed was his, that of bringing home enough money to sustain us all. In those days that was a formidable task.

Things were always right on the edge where money was concerned and he worried constantly about our non-existent finances. At the same time he had so great a love for life that no matter what happened he made it through and with humor and love for his family and his home.

He did have a fierce temper though. And, sometimes he'd explode over almost nothing at all. I remember we had a white cat. A scruffy looking thing that Dad definitely did not like. The only reason he put up with it was because Mom felt sorry for the thing and would put food and water out for it and let it in when the weather was cold. One day Mom had just put dinner on the table and came into the living room to collect Dad and myself. When Dad went into the kitchen he found the cat dining on the venison roast Mom had prepared for dinner. He grabbed the cat by the neck and without a word marched out the back door to the chopping block we had for splitting logs. He picked up the axe threw the cat down on the chopping block and cut its head off right there with Mom and I looking on. That's the most violent I ever saw him.

Usually his explosions were verbal and there was no doubt what he was upset about. I caught hell from him many times, usually for my carelessness or recklessness. I wore glasses from the time I was in the second grade and, of course, I was constantly breaking them, and since money was so precious he would give me hell for doing something stupid. When he was angry he withdrew his love, it seemed to me, and would go inside himself sometimes for days at a time. But, then the storm passed and things would return to normal.

Dad came from a generation that believed that as soon as you were able you went to work. Schooling was frosting on the cake and not really necessary. Although he only had a sixth grade education he continued learning all of his life, he read constantly, and could do math better than I could when I was in high school. He thought going to college was a big waste of money and time and never once did he encourage me to further my education. I think he resented my going to college that first year and still living at home, instead of getting a job and starting to support myself, although I did work for him every chance I got.

Dad never missed work, (when there was any), a day in his life. It took a life threatening illness to keep him from going to work. Even at age 72, when he finally retired, he said to me, "It's not a nice feeling to think you can't support your family anymore." I tried to offer my opinion about the matter saying he had worked hard enough all his life and now it was time to kick back and just enjoy life for a change.

He did finally adjust to retirement. The folks had $1,000 in the bank, Dad had his Social Security, and my brother and I supplemented that little income with $100 a month each; their house was paid for; and Dad thought that they were more secure than they had ever been in their married life. So, he relaxed and enjoyed the next seven years prior to his death.

Day 45.

"...I have a rendezvous with death..."

—Seeger

    ❦   ❦   ❦

Damn, I think I've caught a cold. Last night I had chills alternating with a fever and I feel really lousy today. If a cold is a virus, the Rhinovirus, how in the devil did I get it up here? Maybe it's not a cold, maybe it's the ague, whatever that is. I know people used to get what they called the ague, seems like my folks had it a couple of times when I was growing up. Anyway, whatever I've got it's the pits, I feel like hell.

It shouldn't surprise me. After 44 days in a tree with the damn weather like it has been. No wonder I've got something, for all I know it might be moss. I'm surprised I didn't come down with something sooner than this. Maybe I ought to just go down, crawl into a nice warm bed, and forget that I was so stupid as ever to conceive this idea. Oh, yes, and pay my ersatz friends a thousand bucks. That's the part that really sticks in my craw. Not only having to admit defeat but to award them for being so cocksure that I wouldn't make it. To hell with them. I'll just die up here.

I'm feeling so lousy that I can't think to write anything. So I'm just going to sleep all day and maybe kick this thing.

Day 46.

"When lilacs round the dooryard bloom…"

—Walt Whitman

❈　　　❈　　　❈

I got to wondering, why is a flower? I mean, we try to explain everything so scientifically. Then let me ask, why is a flower a flower? To attract insects so that it can pollinate, science would answer; but surely in the course of evolution nature could have devised other means. And, we know there are numerous ways to attract insects, smell is probably the best way but sitting on your patio at sundown in your shirtsleeves works just as well for mosquitoes. So, there must be thousands of ways Mother Nature could have devised for getting plants to spread their pollen. Instead we have flowers. I wonder is beauty involved in any way? Do insects, especially bees, enjoy the beautiful blossoms spread before them in the Spring and Summer? I never gave that much credit to a bee. The thought just passed through my hazy brain when I looked below and saw a multitude of wild flowers blooming on the floor of the forest. If I were a bee I'd sure enjoy the hell out of it.

It also occurred to me that If the flower is the ultimate in beauty in the plant world surely music is the same in the world of man.

From time to time I remember whole passages from some of my favorite songs and even from some classical pieces. I am able to play them in my mind. Of course, it is just memory but the music is there just the same as if I were hearing it on my CD player. Songs are relatively easy but try remembering and hearing in your mind that grand passage *Liebestod* from Wagner's *Tristan and Isolde*. It is wonderful when I can remember it.

My mind, and for that matter, anybody's mind must be somewhat like a sponge. It soaks up everything that passes through one's senses. It must all be there in your brain somewhere, stored in bits and pieces, that have meaning only if you attempt to remember an incident or a bit of music or a love affair or a scientific fact. What a wonder the human brain. It is so far beyond anything we imagine it to be that I conjecture it will always remain a mystery.

In this regard how does the mind conceive an idea? How does it process words to form a poem? How does it hear music that has yet to be written down? How does it recognize beauty? How does it allow me to indulge in all my nonsense and still keep me sane?

Day 47.

"In the late summer of that year, we lived in a house in a village
that looked across the river and the plains to the mountains."

—Hemmingway

❧   ❧   ❧

Reminiscing again.

My mother was the most wonderful and complete mother one can imagine.
She was sweet, gentle, comforting, encouraging, forgiving; she had all the
attributes a child could want in a mother.

She loved her home. She built her life around that old house and her family
and her belief in God. She had many friends, good, kind women like herself,
mostly associated with the church. But her primary love was my father, her two
boys, and that old house which she made into the most comfortable and welcoming home she possibly could.

She would sew and crochet and with her friends, make quilts out of old
pieces of fabric and hooked rugs from rags. With what few dollars she ever had
she bought pieces of used furniture and old carpets and she would grow plants
and flowers and place them artistically around the house.

She decorated for every holiday. To walk in our front door was to be greeted
by a wonderful display of the holiday, Halloween, Thanksgiving, Christmas,
whatever, on the dining room table, the buffet, the fireplace mantle, and on
every horizontal surface in the living room. It was all wonderful. It was home,
and my mother made it that way.

She had a very hard, very difficult life as a young woman. She was the eldest of eight children, and in effect, she was as much the mother as her mother was in raising the other kids.

From what she told me, she and her family moved to Oklahoma territory where her father participated in the Oklahoma land rush. They had less than nothing and lived in a "soddy," while her father and mother attempted to scratch a living out of that barren soil. Her father really wasn't a farmer and it was clear they couldn't make a go of it farming on the land he had staked out. However, he did have some education, and eventually he went to work for the railroad, and later became Superintendent of Schools in the local district.

Along the way three of her sisters died. Two of them, I think, simply because they were so poor and ill-nourished that disease overwhelmed them easily. The older one was killed in an airplane crash in 1930.

Anyway, my mother became a schoolteacher in a little one-room school-house on the prairie where she taught grades one through six. She must have been 17 or 18 then. It was while she was teaching that she met my father. A year later they were married.

Day 48.

"The end crowns all;
And that old common arbitrator, time,
Will one day end it."

—Shakespeare

❧   ❧   ❧

Not feeling any better but did manage to get some sleep, and after eating a little this morning I think I may live. Trouble is I don't know if I want to if I'm going to continue feeling this badly. I woke up in the middle of the night burning up so I couldn't sleep any more. I started talking to Charlie and we had an interesting conversation, I think. It had something to do with old age and illness and the deterioration of the human body virtually from the time your 30 years old, maybe even before that. Anyway, getting old is not a nice way to end one's life. If I could think of a better way I'd choose it, but if you're reasonably healthy you've probably got to go through it.

Then I remembered something I jotted down after I'd gone on my walk one day. I think it went something like this:

Like everyone else I know, I have days when I get depressed. I'm old, my back aches, and the sky is overcast. I feel miserable and dispirited and at odds with almost everything, and yet I can't single out one thing that is causing me such despair. In my case I blame it on having nothing to do, and yet I have a list of things to do a mile long, and don't want to do any of them.

I just want to stand and stare. There was a poet one time that said, "What is this world so full of care, that we have no time to stand and stare?" And, I seem to remember Mark Twain saying that some of his best thoughts came to him when he was just sitting on a rock staring at nothing in particular. Maybe that's what I need to do, just sit and stare. Maybe there is something lurking in the recesses of my brain that needs defining, needs tying together, comprehension, and understanding. Maybe I am trying desperately to understand myself, or life, or its meaning. Maybe I just need to stare long enough to let my brain process all it knows, or thinks it knows, or better still maybe I just need to stand still, and not try to think, and maybe life will explain itself to me.

I've taken to walking again each day, about a mile I guess. It's not much of a walk. Not much nature to see in a housing development but this one is nice enough. Usually, I'm the only one about, and I listen to the cooing of the pigeons who have made the neighborhood theirs, and occasionally, I see a flight of wild geese moving smoothly overhead amidst all of their chatter.

I have a yellow Labrador Retriever friend who greets me if she is out in her back yard, and I always stop, and let her lick my hand through the fence while I stroke her beautiful head, and scratch behind her ears.

This morning I saw an old man taking his dog for a walk, or vice versa. The dog was out in front, walking slowly with his head down, and the old man, (he could have been my age or even younger), was following along with his head down, too. I couldn't imagine what each of them found so interesting in the sidewalk.

The dog was a greyhound, probably one of those rescued from the dog track after it's useful life had been exhausted chasing a phony rabbit around a track for the amusement and financial risk of a band of spectators who didn't give a damn about the dogs except as winners or losers.

I thought, what had that dog's life been about. He'd raced, what? Maybe a hundred, hundred and fifty times, and the rest of the time he'd been cooped up in a three by four foot cage with an old blanket for a bed, and maybe, if he was lucky and had a good owner, he was allowed some exercise and some freedom from his cage ever so often. But, probably, because he had been bred to run and all his genes were programmed so that the only time he lived, really lived, he was running, in a pack of his fellows, after a mechanical rabbit that whirled around a mechanical track, while cheers, encouragements, and imprecations roared from another pack of animals who had congregated to watch his, and the others of his kind, their moments of life.

As I watched that old man, and that old retired greyhound, both with their heads down staring at nothing but the sidewalk, and what was in their mind's eye, I wondered if that isn't what all life is, just moments when we feel like we are living, just moments when there is exhilaration, exuberance, beauty in movement, or in what one is witnessing, when life seems vibrant, and important, and real.

Then, I thought, maybe that's all there is to it, for all of us, we get born, we live our programmed lives, and then we get old, and remember the times of our lives when we lived, really lived, while we stare at the sidewalk, walking an old dog, who, for all we know, is doing the same thing, remembering.

God, I'm sick. I hope I live through the night.

Day 49.

"I look into those dear dumb eyes,
And wonder where the difference lies
Between my soul and thine."

—Unknown

❧   ❧   ❧

Talking about that old Greyhound started me thinking about the greatest dog in the world, Butch. He and I grew up together from the time I was eight until I went into military service when I was just about to have my eighteenth birthday. He was my best friend.

Butch spent the nights, most of the time, at home but during the day when I was in school, and then only when the teachers barred him from laying quietly in the aisle beside my seat, he was off roaming, usually with Rex his black, none-too-friendly friend. The two dogs played at mock battles with one another, searched garbage cans for food, chased after any females in heat, scared the chickens that some folks kept in backyards, and once or twice, wandered far enough out into the country to chase some sheep. Some farmer's shotgun discouraged them sufficiently to keep that recreation at a minimum.

Out on North Avenue where the dogs roamed daily was Curnow's Frozen Food Lockers. It was a big building that housed a large cold storage room with rows of two-foot square lockers where people mainly kept frozen meat. In the Fall all the town's deer or elk hunters would bring their kill to Curnow's for butchering, wrapping into meal size portions, quick-freezing, and storing in the rented lockers.

There were about a dozen people doing the butchering and because of his frequent begging visits they all got to know Butch. They would save scraps and bones for him and would pass them through the screen door to him almost daily. Butch was very appreciative of the handouts and would warmly waggle and voice his appreciation in a peculiar croon that clearly was a "thank you."

Because of the many flies and other insects gathered at the screen door where Butch was fed, the meat cutters installed a small sliding door in the lower half of a window above a cutting table. Very quickly Butch discerned that the little door was for him and the routine became one of his rearing up so he was visible in the window over the sliding door, giving one or two loud announcements of his presence, then accepting the gifts offered through the little door.

Shortly, Butch began showing up at the window twice in rapid succession each day. Each time the cutters gave him scraps but they knew that he could not possibly consume more than the quantity given him at his first appearance. So, on the third or fourth day of this ritual after giving him the first of his two rations one of the meat cutters followed him and watched as Butch carried the large, meat-laden bone he had just received across the street to where Rex lay comfortably on a green lawn in the shade of a Cottonwood tree. Butch dropped the bone between Rex's paws, barked once, and turned back to Curnow's for what was obviously to be his share of the take.

Who says animals don't think and deeply? I sure wish Butch was up here with me. He'd be a hell of a lot more company than Charlie.

Day 50.

"And lose the name of action."

—Shakespeare

❦　　❦　　❦

Happy halfway through my latest insanity. Fifty days in a tree. I should be committed.

I'm still sick but I made it through the night. Isn't there a song like that, "...help me make it through the night." I wish someone would. I haven't eaten much the past two days and I think I'm getting weak. I'd better stop and fix myself something.

(Later)

I spent most of the day sleeping and really woke up about sundown. I think I feel a little better. Still somewhat feverish, but better overall. While lying in that kind of twilight sleep even then I was writing. It all made very good sense to me until I started to write it down. Then I wasn't sure I even knew what the hell I was talking about. Anyway, I think it was something like this:

The two biggest regrets of my life are that I was too young for World War II and too old for the sexual revolution. I was ten when the United States finally got into WWII, and I remember so well how desperately I wanted to be in that war.

Looking back on it, it was the perfect war, if there can be such a thing. We had the perfect enemy, Adolph Hitler, who epitomized the very essence of evil, the personification of the devil himself. It was perfectly clear to the whole world that Chancellor Hitler and his allies, especially Japan, wanted to destroy us all and have things their own way. It was equally obvious to a ten-year-old boy that it was a war of survival and that we must all fight if we were going to win. I just had to wait my chance.

Unfortunately my chance never came so I was forced to grow up during the war and then find myself too late and remorseful, at age 15, destined to live in a peacetime world, where good enemies were hard to find and where our advancing technology did not bode well for future engagements.

I have since evolved a theory about enemies. As I said good ones now-a-days are hard to find, and I believe that good enemies are absolutely indispensable to the good health of a nation. A good enemy causes a focus of attention, a direction for our innate animosity toward one another, someone to blame for things going wrong, a fall guy who can be blamed for everything from a constantly increasing national budget to why life is so tough and prices so high. And, with a good war, we feel free to indulge ourselves almost without restriction, throw away our inhibitions, and loosen the reins on our moderation.

Without good enemies a nation inevitably starts chewing on itself and we fight amongst ourselves over petty issues that seem to multiply like mice in a laboratory. Sports help. We can divert ourselves momentarily with physical contests where we play out a miniature war between teams of large, over-paid athletes, having chosen one team as the "good" guys.

But this is no way to live. Where is the drama, the pathos, the living close to death day-by-day. It's when we do live close to death that we really live. Otherwise why would we do all those stupid things we do like hang-gliding, mountain climbing, sky-diving, iron-man marathons, car racing, or eating all those high cholesterol, high fat, high salt, high sugar, tasty foods that we love so dearly. Ah, well. Maybe I did miss the big war but I've surely been involved with the all too numerous little wars with myself that life seems to have awarded me.

Day 51.

"Shall I say, I have gone at dusk through narrow streets,
And watched the smoke that rises from the pipes
Of lonely men in shirtsleeves, leaning out of windows?..."

—T. S. Eliot

❧   ❧   ❧

I still don't feel worth a damn. It's hard to continue up here but I'm still determined to do it. I know it's foolish but I'm an old man. If I weren't doing this what else would I be doing? And, when it's over I'll have the knowledge that I did it, which isn't really all that significant, but, who knows, I may have gained some other knowledge besides. Siddhartha sat and meditated for a longer time than I'll be in this tree and look what happened to him.

I was thinking about words and how much I love them. They are so wonderful because in the words of the famous semanticist Alfred Habdank Skarbek Korzybski, "The word is not the thing." So, you can use words all you want and they are only words. They may not mean anything to anyone but you; they may offend those with delicate ears; they may be used to sway crowds; they may be used to promote politics, or religion, or commerce, or anything under the sun, but they are only words and as we all know, words have a way of disappearing once they have been said. They are whispers in the wind. Which reminds me of a poem written by my favorite of all cartoonists, Walt Kelly. I think it goes like this:

There's a star in the wind and the wind winds high,
Blowing alight thru fog, thru night
Thru cold, thru cold and the bitter alone…
There high in the wind rides a Star, my own,
And the Star is a Word…of white…of white,
And the star in the wind is a Word.

I've no idea what that means, if indeed it means anything at all, but I love the rhythm and the feel of it, and even if it doesn't mean anything, it is a still a thing of beauty for there is music in those words.

How in the world did I remember, "Alfred Habdank Skarbek Korzybski?" Must come from the days when I studied semantics and Korzybski is foremost in that field, besides, how many people do I know with a name like Habdank or Skarbek. It's one of those things that just gets stuck in my brain. I can't help it. It's a flaw in my character.

Here's a poem I wrote about words:

Why these words
To say the things I feel?

Why these issues of sound
At every instance,
To describe the action,
Rather than to act?

Why, must my thinking,
Be transformed into words,
Even though the thought has passed
And the word's no longer necessary?

Words are more than feelings,
And say too much,
And carry with them,
Germs of their antithesis.

Why must I say "I love you,"
When you know it and I know it,
And love is inexpressible in words.

And love hides hate within itself,
As life hides death,
And God, goddamn.

All words hide simple feelings,
Insidiously run the world,
And hide us from ourselves.

Day 52.

"...I'm singing, just singing in the rain."

❦   ❦   ❦

I'm not great but significantly better. The fever has diminished to where I just seem to glow a little but the chills have stopped, thank goodness. It's raining again, goddamn it. There were several nice days when I was too sick to enjoy them. Now it's back to the same old thing, day after stupid day. It's like the guy in California when asked about the weather said: "Just one goddamned nice day after another." Except in my case you could delete the "nice" part.

When you really stop to consider love, it turns out to be a very complex and confusing subject.

I've always had trouble with the differences we all seem to imply when we use the word, *love*. The differences between love for our lovers, our spouses, our mother, father, children, life. Is love a subjective quality? It's all love isn't it?

Maybe love is a universal quality and it simply becomes distorted by the way we use the word. To say we love our parents means something entirely different than how we love our children. There are elements of respect and longevity and childhood and memory all mixed together in parental love. Its different with children although the *quality* of the love itself is the same.

Somehow we understand these differences when we speak of love but does that make the love itself different? It seems to be the context that changes. I am inclined to believe that we love the people and the things we say we love genuinely but we subjectivize this universal feeling to fit our own definition and our own perception of the object we say we love.

Love is another of the many personal projections of our selves. But the concept of love; the semantical definition of the word allows for no variation—love is love. It is only our application of the word that signifies differences. It is those things underlying our use of the word that make the difference. Things like lust, respect, greed, relationship, memory, awe of beauty, selfishness, self-indulgence, or pretence, which colors our use of the word. These things are *not* love. They only condition the word to fit what we consider to be our many loves.

I guess what I'm trying to say is the word is pure; it is _love_, regardless of its application. It is only used or misused through our subjective ideas of what it means and the intensity in which we use the term. This intensity changes with respect to the object referenced. For example, the feeling associated with love for a spouse is much different than that expressed for "love of mankind." Or the love of a material object. Further, there is the aspect of time involved for surely love changes as we change over time. The intense youthful (and lustful) love we feel for our spouse at the time of getting married changes as both of you age. It can become more or less but nonetheless, it changes. The love for your children also becomes different as they leave home and develop their own lives which are not so intimately involved with your own.

We have come to use the word "love" so frequently and indiscriminately that it has lost much of its meaning. We love art, we love music, we love a car (I personally love Jaguar coupes), we love our wife, children, parents, aunts, uncles, animals, chocolate, certain foods, sports, etc., etc., etc. We apply the term to anything and everything.

Maybe, in one sense, it is good that we love so freely and are able to feel so intensely about people or things that we can apply such a strong term to our feelings for so many things.

On the other hand, perhaps, its too frequent use has so diluted the word and the feelings behind it that it is no longer the same term used by songwriters and poets through the ages. Maybe it has grown hackneyed through too much, indeed overmuch usage to the point where it means little, if anything.

I would not like to think that the latter is the case.

Day 53.

"Once more unto the breach dear friends..."

—Shakespeare

*   *   *

I think life is truly remarkable for it somehow prepares you for the future albeit most often not in very pleasant ways. I think that the carrying of a child in the womb for nine months prepares a mother for birth. And the rearing of a child, especially during the teenage years, prepares parents for the time when the child leaves home,(boy, does it ever!) and conversely, the surge of hormones in the child prepares them to leave and take up life on their own.

Certainly life prepares one for old age. The diminution of strength, sex drive, ambition, all prepare one for a quieter life much as a clock spring unwinds and grows weaker as it expends its energy impelling a pendulum. But, it is the transition that is difficult because your head tells you one thing and your body tells you another. In my mind I am still 35 and I see the world from eyes in a face that is not wrinkled and sagging but from the face of myself that I have carried within me all my years.

And, in my mind's eye, I see all of the things that need doing or that I want to do, and I may even try doing them but then a random pain, a shortness of breath, a cramping in a muscle brings to me the realization that I am old, parts of me have worn down, lost strength, diminished in mass and tone, that some of my past physical exertions have damaged parts of me and now that damage comes to call on me in the form of aching shoulders and an untrustworthy back. I hate this aging process. It's very unpleasant and not only that, it doesn't fit into my plan of not dying.

Try as I might to see myself as I really am, in my subconscious I am still a young man wanting to feel all of the life and do all of the wonderful things that are offered to the young. Perhaps, one day I will succeed in bringing myself up-to-date but for the time being I can only look backward and re-live those days when I was indestructible and mortality was not even a consideration.

I am a complete reprobate for I want back the sex, the drinking, the carousing around with disreputable friends. I want to dissipate again with wine, women and song. I want to party and get drunk and engage in carnal activity with lovely young women and go skiing and hiking and hunting and run with the wild ones. But, alas, that is behind me and all I can do now is remember how much fun it was.

Is it my soul or its flesh
That is crying?

Does my soul weep
For its lost freedom,
Or the joy it once knew
In the thrill of youth?

Or is it this temporal husk,
With its waning light,
That, remembering, feels
Its diminished stature,
And, remarking on its past
And future course,
Speculates upon its worth?

Day 54.

❦   ❦   ❦

I guess I'm better. I'm still not up to par but I no longer think I'm dying. I eat okay but I still feel weak and jittery. I wanted to write today because I thought of something that I believe deserves a few words. Here they are:

GOD IN A BOX

I had a friend once who, he thought, was a very good Christian. Now I don't profess to know one way or the other but to me he was a pure and simple hypocrite. He was intensely intelligent but at the same time gravely ignorant. There is a difference you know. He had the intelligence to know more than he did but he was so sure he was right that he refused to think beyond what he believed.

His beliefs were very traditional, very orthodox, and very bigoted. He knew, for example, that everything in the Bible was literally true. Not analogy, not metaphor, not simile, not allegory, but plain and simple literal truth. Now, I must confess that I do not agree with that definition of the Bible. As a matter of fact I have a great deal of trouble with the word "Truth" itself. But, that is beside the point.

My friend, I am sure, has always regarded me as a heretic, and I am also sure that he probably thinks of me going to hell and burning there, along with all the other non-believers in the world, throughout history. Hell must be a crowded place.

How he could associate with me I never quite figured out. Maybe it was his Christian charity.

To get to my point, I was considering one day, his view of God, and according to what I know of him and his orthodox views, he must believe that God is a supreme being, in the shape of man, because God made man in his own image. God is male. He is a jealous God. He reigns in heaven, wherever that is, among all of his angels. He is beneficent to those who worship him, attend church, undergo ritual, praise him in prayer, song, and tithes, and who acknowledge his son as the savior of mankind and the one and only path to heaven.

Since my friend believes in all of this, he considers himself "saved," while anyone who believes differently is destined to hell. His is a simple and self-serving faith because he knows he is "right" and all of us other poor devils are just plain "wrong."

He is very satisfied with his beliefs. He has worked it all out so that his God is the only God, and since he is on such intimate terms with God, he does not need to question the truth or the factualness of his beliefs. He has defined God to suit his beliefs. He has put God in a box of his own manufacture. How convenient. In his case, rather than say, "God created man in his own image," maybe it should be "I created God in my image."

I don't mean to belittle my friend or his beliefs. They are his beliefs and that's who he is. But I dislike closed-minded people. It is such a shame that they cannot open up to see a world unlike the one they have constructed in their head. To see all the many different philosophies, and theologies, and religions, and spiritual ideas in the world. Granted they may hold little more credence than the one my friend believes, but it does give one the opportunity to examine some options in selecting what we choose to believe. To choose one dogma from the beginning of one's life and not investigate alternatives to that dogma seems to me to be a denial of the possibilities of God. I also happen to believe that learning is the meaning of life and if one denies the opportunity to learn, one is denying life.

My friend is still my friend and I staunchly defend his right to believe whatever he wishes. I just wish he could do the same for me without sending me to hell.

Day 55.

"O Freedom! Thou art not as poets dream"

—William C. Bryant

❋ ❋ ❋

I guess because my freedom is so constrained, I have been thinking a lot about freedom. I think it is both a blessing and a curse, like so much else in human existence. Being born and raised, and continuing as an adult in the United States, I never questioned my freedom. I took it all for granted. We have a constitution that guarantees our freedoms and they are many. It is only when one goes to a foreign country, particularly Asian near-eastern or far-eastern countries, that freedom is brought home forcibly to one raised in the U. S.

The laws of other countries generally do not pay much attention to the rights of the individual, it is the state that is important, and the laws are not so much for protection of the populace as they are for making sure the populace conforms to the demands of the state.

However, there is danger in freedom. Thirty or more years ago I read a book, called something like, "The Decline of Democracy." The author pointed out that the seeds of destruction are intricately woven into the fabric of democracies in the form of freedoms. I thought about that and I think that author, whose name I can't remember, is absolutely right. Take Freedom of Speech for example. In a government-dominated and controlled society, speech is closely monitored for there is power in words. Control of the press, radio, TV, and every other medium of expression are absolutely necessary, if the power of the state is to remain absolute.

Also, Freedom of Speech, in a truly free society is a double-edged sword. In classic human behavior, there are those who will abuse their freedom, and turn it toward a low money making proposition such as the sale of pornography over the Internet. But, one cannot condone one type of speech and condemn another, if speech is truly free.

Day 56.

"O rally 'round the flag, boys, rally once again,
Shouting the battle cry of Freedom."

—G. F. Root

❧   ❧   ❧

Yesterday's entry got me to thinking about censorship? I know that some schools, perhaps many or all of them, will not allow certain books in their libraries. I can understand the protection of the minds of children in that regard. However, proper censorship rests in the minds of those who are doing the censoring. If the censor is biased, (and show me someone who isn't), that bias will show through clearly in what that person censors. And, where does that sort of thing stop? You begin with censoring smut and you end up censoring great literature or children's books.

Another point, I understand that some of the books removed or really never entered into school libraries are banned because of sexual content, or violence, or naughty words. Well, if my high school days were any criteria, you can forget the sexual content prohibition, even in my day there were no secrets about intimate male/female relationships. Sex was and still is the most popular subject and pastime that old Mom Nature ever invented. Hell, they even teach sex in school now so just what is it the librarians are afraid of? Romance?

As for violence, first turn off the TV, and remove all the video games from all the stores and the hands of the children, then, and only then, can you think about removing the least offensive of these entertainments, books.

With regard to naughty words, I submit that there is not a dirty word or a swear word that is not being used frequently by most children by the time they are 10, or 12 at the outside. If they themselves do not use such words they most certainly hear them constantly coming from their friends if not their family. TV is another good source for expanding one's vocabulary in the field of the vulgar. But, back to old Korzybski, "the word is not the thing." They are only words. It is our individual judgment of them that makes them naughty, vulgar, in bad taste, or not fit for our children's ears. I think those kind of judgments are wrong, stupid, and ineffective. Like it or not our children will hear the words, and read the books, and see the movies that we do not endorse. In this case our children are smarter than we. The fact is, to a free people censorship is abhorrent. It is clearly a case of setting up someone to be the authority on what is and what is not acceptable in a society. My writings probably would never make the acceptable list. I hope not.

This establishment of authority will not stop with censorship. It will ultimately extend to every aspect of what is proper in a proper society, such as speech, writing, poetry, religion, politics, teaching, clothing, hair cuts, etc., etc. In short, the act of limiting freedom of speech in a society is tantamount to the compromise of every freedom, and in such a society, democracy will cease to be.

Day 57.

"In a noisy world
Being slightly deaf
Is a blessing."

—RRR

❋   ❋   ❋

Still thinking about free speech and censorship, I fantasized myself back in the mid-1700s speaking against the puritanical advocacy of censorship. This is what I would have said:

"The censoring of intellectual material of any kind at the sole discretion of a self-appointed group of supposed moral experts is the grossest infringement of individual rights and clearly contrary to the high ideals contributing to the establishment of these colonies. The tyranny expressed in such censorship is characteristic of the despotism from which we have ostensibly only recently escaped. If we indeed have not escaped but only succeeded in establishing its facsimile in this remote and beautiful land, then we are worse than those who practice such evils in that place from whence we came. For we, having the opportunity to do better, fail even to do something new, and so set in motion for ourselves and our children the same iniquities, the same injustice, and the same oppression which we eschewed and vowed never to imitate. If this be the course we have elected to pursue, I for one will not accede, and will, insofar as I am able, continue to act as a free man with all the rights and privileges attendant thereto."

Ha! How about that for a stentorian speech? I should have been a states-man. In the 1700s, of course.

Day 58.

"…make my knees callous,
Cultivate a supple spine,
Wear out my belly groveling in the dust?

No thank you."

—Rostand

❧   ❧   ❧

The free speech that I wrote about yesterday is largely the political side of freedom. The religious side is something else altogether.

The best treatise on religious freedom I have ever read is the one in *The Brothers Karamazov*, where Ivan concocts the play, *The Grand Inquisitor*. In Ivan's play the Grand Inquisitor of Spain speaks to Christ about the freedom he promised the people, and the futility of such a promise. As I recall, the Inquisitor says something to the effect that because of that promise it has taken the church fifteen centuries to get mankind back under control (i.e. that is the control of the Church).

The Inquisitor insists that mankind is base and brutal and has little use for freedom. Man wants to be controlled, and if he thinks that control emanates from a higher power then he will gladly submit, especially if there are secular benefits to be had by that submission. "Feed men, and then ask of them virtue!" was the Inquisitor's advice to Christ. Freedom he says in so many words, does not fill bellies.

There is more truth than fantasy in *The Grand Inquisitor* for a lot of mankind does not even recognize freedom as necessary to a good life. They are perfectly happy if their secular desires are satisfied by whatever means and under whatever religious or political system they may find themselves. Freedom is a construct of many elements, speech, religion, politics, safety, and the flexibility to move freely from place to place without restriction. Some people may feel that, to preserve some of these elements, it is acceptable to deny others.

It is a deep subject, one I have only begun to examine thoroughly. I may not live long enough to understand it.

A friend once in reflective mood,
Said, "Looking back I wish
I'd made something of myself."

"Really?" I responded,
"What would you have made?"

How strange the things in life
We think may mean success,
Especially when once achieved
We find them not at all,
What we had presupposed.
Disillusioned, we set other goals,
And so continue striving,
To give our lives some meaning.

Once, I understand, it was not so,
Being born meant predestination,
In a world of men
Where fathers or divine dispensation,
Determined what and how we were,
And precluded speculation.

Then Freedom struck our hearts and minds,
And tore away the judgment of a God
Condemning men, like glowing stars,
To fixed positions.

But, as if to chastise naughty children,
We were left free to choose,
Without a guide,
The path to what our self-enfeebled eyes,
Presumed to be a lofty mountaintop,
Only to find, once we had climbed,
That freedom had eluded us.

The top achieved,
And ready for grand vistas,
We only found ourselves
Still earthbound.

Day 59.

❦   ❦   ❦

Another thing about freedom. I've wanted to get this off my chest for a long time. It's about smoking. I smoked cigarettes for 40 years, and although I quit years ago, I guess I'm still a smoker at heart because whenever I hear or read that the campaign against smoking has taken away another freedom I burn, and smoke, inside.

I very well know that democracy is synonymous with "Rule of the majority." But I also seem to remember that this great country was founded on "Liberty" which I have always interpreted as: the right to do as one pleases. Oh, I know, that the health risks have enabled the repression of smoking in public and I don't disagree entirely, in public buildings, O.K.; in restaurants, O.K.; in public transportation, O.K.; but in bars? This gives me serious heartburn. And, in the open air? Come on. This is taking the public's health to an illogical extreme. It has become much like "National Security," where any constraint is justifiable if it impedes or jeopardizes "National Security." Where does this curtailment of personal freedom end?

Under the aegis of saving us from the enemy, (which is now defined to include tobacco), government, be it city, county, state, or federal, can close down any of our freedoms and explain it away as national security or health hazard or danger to the majority. What about the minority? Have they no voice in this? What has happened to their liberty? Is it to be denied so that the majority, in all its wisdom, can suspend this or that group's liberty whenever it does not match their idea of what's proper, or good for you, or objectionable?

Under this premise, let us demand the end of violence, and bad language, and nudity in the movies and on TV. Let us deny the rights of all those who drive too fast or run yellow lights at intersections or drive recklessly. Let us withdraw liberty from those who participate in sports for surely that is dangerous to themselves and others who participate. Let us crack down on the coffee drinkers, the chocolate abusers, the pizza lovers, and the French fryers. Let us rebuke those who would speak against the government for aren't they clearly speaking against the majority who elected the officials who run that government?

Don't tell me what's good for me. I already know that tobacco can and probably does cause cancer and I shouldn't smoke because I might be at risk.

Isn't that my business? I am an educated person, and certainly I have witnessed all of the no smoking campaigns since J. Everett Koop first voiced his opinion. But don't tell me that I have to give up something I enjoy, regardless of whether or not it may kill me, to serve the greater ideal of the majority. I'm supposed to be a free citizen in a free country "…with liberty and justice for all." And, as for doing something that will kill me, tell that to all the people who indulge in alcohol, in fast food, in high impact sports, or dangerous games. Tell it to those who climb Mount Everest, or wrestle alligators, or ride bicycles, or motorcycles, or drive cars.

We make a mockery of ourselves when we go on crusades for one thing or another. In the process we kill off our freedoms, and draw closer to a severely regulated and dictatorial nation, even if the dictator is the "Majority."

Day 60.

"A poet that reads his verse in public
may have other nasty habits."

—Heinlein

❧   ❧   ❧

I'm on a poetry binge...I don't feel well...I'm depressed...I'm lonely...I want to go home and be with my lovely wife...I talk to her in my poetry...I hope she can hear me.

Come walk with me,
And we will find a patch of green,
With sky and cloud,
And one tall tree,
And we will leave behind
All that we are,
All our words and answers,
All of our trite history,
All we know, and have known.
Let us start from here.
Come, walk with me.

❦   ❦   ❦

Had I but choice,
I would subdue the poet in me,
For it mocks my every move,
And tempts me toward recklessness.

It is an idiot child,
Tantrum-filled,
Questioning meanings,
Demeaning motives,
Abrogating seriousness.

Disdaining high endeavors,
It seeks only freedom,
Amidst green fields,
Filled with laughter and music,
And wild flowers,
And quiet moments,
Accompanied only by my Love.

Day 61.

"I am not mad; I would to heaven I were;
For then, 'tis like I should forget myself…"

—Shakespeare

❧　　　❧　　　❧

I've had a relapse…I'm sick as hell…the fever has returned…I'm losing weight…I can't think straight…everything is a jumble…I want a cigarette…I know I quit a long time ago but now, at this moment, I want a damn cigarette…and, I'm out of scotch…I'm in a hell of a mess.

I've thought of myself lately as doing something akin to the Lakota Sundance except for the skewering of my pectorals and hanging around the teepee until I blessedly go unconscious. However, with that slight exception I have surely been meditating and hallucinating all over the 80 square feet of my living space. Maybe it isn't so much the same after all. But, bizarre, I know it is.

Only thirty-nine days left to go. I hope I don't die before they get me down. I'd like to feel earth again and a bed and clean sheets and dry clothes and hot food, and, and, and. God I hate it up here. I pray to God that if I ever think of doing anything this crazy again that he/she/it sends a lightning bolt to incinerate me on the spot before I can take the first step.

What the hell's going on in the world? I've lost all contact. Which, if I remember correctly, is just what I wanted to do.

None of us realize what it is to be completely cut off from all of mankind. It is the worst fate I can imagine. The only thing that has kept me going the past two months is the thought that it would soon be over. If a person was sentenced to this isolation for very long, I can't imagine not finding some way to exterminate yourself.

I feel light-headed and giddy. I tried doing some deep thinking but it didn't work. I can't seem to get my thoughts in order. Did I write about *The Grand Inquisitor*? I think I did but I can't remember what I wrote or why. I hammered out a poem last night before the fever got me again.

Often, when time illuminates
My past,
I feature I have lived
A dream,
Of someone else's manufacture.

It is as though
I've tread upon a path,
Directed by an unseen hand,
That subtly steers my course,
And lets me ponder why and how
I've come by such a way.

By fascination,
A wanderer driven,
Marveling at miracles
Constantly around and inside me.

Awe-stricken,
Enamored of life and Earth,
I was easily led.

Whether genes or culture,
Or a dreamer's vision,
I know not,
And little difference
Does it make,
I've lived enthralled by life

And never would
Have had it otherwise.

Time-wandering in my mind,
I see a dream surreal,
That leads beyond myself,
Before and after,
Then through me,
An awak'ning consciousness,
A desire to confirm reality.

It doesn't make much sense to me now. But then a lot of my poetry doesn't when I read it over again.

Day 62.

"The world may be divided into people that read,
people that write, people that think,
and fox hunters."

—Shenstone

🍁　　　🍁　　　🍁

I have a friend, I call "the Mic." He's a good guy. He edits some of my stuff so that ought to tell how good a friend he is. He voluntarily subjects himself to the ravings of a mad man. Of course, he's a little mad himself so it's "The blind leading the blind." He goes fishing a lot, in a kayak, of all things. Now who the hell can fish from a kayak. I have trouble fishing from a yacht, and to tell the truth I'd really rather not fish at all.

Getting back to Mic, he and I used to have some fun times discussing everything from fish, which I'd rather not, to Sartre's existentialism. He and I never agreed on anything, and that's what made it so much fun. We'd sit around the dinner table after a couple of stiff scotches, (neat, no water please), eat and drink wine, and talk in vibrant tones until the wee hours. God, I miss those times.

It occurred to me that true friends should never agree on philosophy. If they do then it's like talking to one's self and what the hell can you learn that way. It's like my talking to Charlie. I state my opinion and he takes the opposite view. Even though it's still me, at least, I allow myself the luxury of questioning my original viewpoint. Sometimes, believe it or not, I actually recognize something that I hadn't thought of before. Maybe I can learn something from Charlie.

My wife and I talk every morning. We have what we call our "fifteen minutes," where we sit in the bedroom, and she drinks her tea and I my coffee, and we ask each other what we think, to which I usually answer, if she gets to the question first, "I think we ought to move right along." A non sequitur to open the conversation. Anyway, we talk about everything, the stuff that concerns us, and the stuff that does not. It usually runs a lot longer than 15 minutes. It keeps us in touch.

I feel a little woozy. I think I'll lie down.

'Tis that first footfall on the path,

'Tis that first line,

That leads from this day to the last,

That stirs the heart,

And captivates the mind,

That lingers in the mem'ry

As the noblest,

That poets perpetuate in rhyme,

'Tis that first moment,

The idea,

That stays and starts the world,

And drives the fatality of time.

Day 63.

❉   ❉   ❉

I got a lot of sleep yesterday and last night. I feel better but I'm still light-headed, and my nose is all stuffed up. In this sorry condition, I wrote this:

Within this smaller orb
Wherein I perceive the larger,
Dwells a little soul,
Narrow in vision,
(Though beholding a world),
Fixed in belief,
(Though questioning always),
Restricted in movement,
(Though constantly in motion),
Stifled, seeking, alone,
While worlds turn,
And Lilacs bloom,
And the rent comes due.

"Come be my love,"
And stop this gnawing
On the bones
And the dry, dead flesh,
Of all the world's inconsequence.

Again restore my lost illusion,
And for one brief moment,
Keep me from myself.

❀   ❀   ❀

It dawned on me that we all live our lives in fragments separated from the rest of the world by our race, our profession, our religion, our location, and probably several other factors. By fragments I mean the little groups of whatever race you happen to belong to. I know that within cities there are small communities of Poles, Russians, Jews, Afro-Americans, Vietnamese, Chinese, Japanese, and on and on. Moreover, beyond the racial separation there is the professional segregation that we voluntarily cling to. Doctors mingle with other doctors, lawyers with lawyers, engineers with other engineers, and then, of course, there is the company society where you confine yourself to the place and people with whom you work. Also, the various technical disciplines such as biology, anthropology, mathematics, paleontology, and all the other 'ologies. People in these fields consort with others in their field. They form their own little segment of society.

The amazing part of all of this is that these little fragments exist side-by-side but yet they are really separate communities. They even have their own languages. The technical language used by biologists is certainly different from that used by engineers or mathematicians. The world of academia is a sterling example of this fragmentation because even in one university you will have many different schools of thought and language and this separation of groups of people even though they are all members of the same larger organization.

How astounding it is that we all assume that everyone is on the same planet as we are, even though it is quite evident that we all exist in our own little universes in our own little realities with others of our subjective family.

Day 64.

"…they also serve who only stand and wait."

—Milton

❈　　　❈　　　❈

I've been remembering my mother taking care of me when I was sick when I was a kid. She hovered over me, fixed me "Mustard Plasters," green tea and toast, and made sure that I was always comfortable. She was a wonderful mother.

In spite of her struggle during her young life or maybe because of it, she always seemed to see the good part of people and any good that could be had from any situation. She loved life, she loved her family, and she loved God. She had faith, more faith, than anyone I have ever known. She once wrote on the flysheet in a book of poetry she gave me on my birthday the verse of Tennyson's that I think describes her better than anything I could ever say. It was: 'Kind hearts are more than coronets, and simple faith than Norman blood.'

She always believed things would turn out all right. I swear I think it was that faith that got the family through some of our most difficult times. She was our anchor, our unfailing strength. She nurtured and cared for each one of us no matter what our trials and tribulations. She was always constant, always there for us, the rock we clung to through all of our troubles. She was our center and all of us circulated around her and home. She never gave way. She was the heart and soul of our small family and she carried that responsibility with a grace and an imperturbability that was nothing short of heroism. We all worshipped her.

My time-tinged mind
Grows heavy with my knowledge,
Constantly sorting through
The trash-heap of my memories,
To construct my future fears.

Life seems so trite and trifling now,
Hackneyed from too much use,
Lacking joy and adventure.

Closed, quiet and ridiculous,
A dry mind in a dry sack.

Day 65.

"...I had a million daydreams to keep me satisfied."

—Song—Gordon Lightfoot

❦　　　❦　　　❦

My childhood was about as good as it could get. Maybe I rant and rave about freedom so much because I had so much when I was a child. From the time I was about eight years old, I was a free spirit. The folks never really placed any limitations on me and the town I grew up in was as safe as any place could be. We never locked the house; left keys in the ignition of the car, at home or downtown; never heard of a case of kidnapping or child molestation. It was a perfect place and a perfect time to be a kid.

It wasn't until my gonads dropped and my testosterone overcame my good sense that I became a little difficult, but by and large I was a good kid.

I got to thinking of my growing years, mainly after I entered puberty and then grew into a young man, and left home.

I am convinced that my young life
Was so strange,
Because I was born in a bowl.

A bowl with mountains for sides,
And me right in the middle,
Like a cornflake or a grape-nut.

The mountains elevated
But restricted my vision,
So that all I ever wanted
Was to look beyond them.

I was sure, you see,
That outside my bowl the world,
Was all I could imagine,
Or hope for,
And that the outside people,
Must be a different race,
Whom I could only hope to emulate.

Older, I breached the walls,
And found the world outside
Not at all what I had thought,
Though round it was,
It bore no other similarity,
To all my preconceptions.

And before too long,
I found my wishing,
Turned back upon itself,
Longing for the womb-like bowl,
And the other cornflakes
Whom I had left behind.

But the bowl was not
What I remembered,
And my newfound outside world,
Was not what I had dreamed.

So I was caught betwixt
My remembrance of that
Which likely never was,
And that which could not be.

And in this place between
Memory and dreams,
I made my own reality,
Adjusted myself to fit,
And let momentum suffice
As life.

Day 66.

"Who am I?
What am I doing here?"

—Ross Pereau's running mate

❧   ❧   ❧

Getting better every day. I'm on the mend, finally. I'm still weak and shaky but the fever has gone and I'm able to get a good night's sleep.

My wife and daughter were out today, using the bullhorn as usual, trying to coax me down and telling me how much they missed me and wanted me safe at home. I liked those words. So much so that I was sorely tempted to tell them to have my son-in-law come get me. Again I held off, but I did say I missed them too, and it wouldn't be much longer until I could hold and kiss them both. I really miss them terribly.

Have you ever noticed how much women talk? They must be the best communicators in the world. When I went on my walks in the morning, nearly always a couple of women would come jogging along chattering to one another all the way. They never stopped even when they were breathing heavy. Their voices filled the air with chirping sounds overlapping one another and interspersed with slight laughter at intervals. It amazed me that they could understand each other for they seemed to be talking at the same time. Maybe understanding wasn't necessary. It was the talking that was important.

My wife can stay on the phone with my daughter for an hour or more, even though they had just talked a couple of days ago, also for an hour or more. Me,

I can't stand telephones and my limit is about three minutes for any phone call. I never even did it when I was a teenager. It always seemed silly to me. I always assumed the telephone was an instrument for conveying a message, not for conversing on everything from little Michael's potty training to NASA's latest space shot. After three minutes I get something akin to "Artillery Ear."

It's a fact, women love to talk; they practice talking; when in the company of other women they cannot help but talk. It is part of their character and they enjoy the hell out of being true to it.

Day 67.

"…a kiss to the beads that brim in the cup,
and a laugh for the foam spilt over,"

—Anon

❧　　　❧　　　❧

Speaking of women yesterday got Charlie and me into a discussion of sex. I have always been a big advocate of sex on every occasion, in every situation, and location. Not that I can pursue that passion anymore. I'm afraid my poor back and lame libido doesn't give me much incentive to play at carnal delights. So, there again I can only look backward to the days of my youth until about 60 to where I was actively engaged in the appreciation of women.

As a young man, women thrilled and excited me from the days even before puberty, although I wasn't quite sure why. After I learned why, they were even more titillating, so to speak.

However, sex as such is an interesting subject. To be thoroughly enjoyable I think there has to be an element of love in the act. Otherwise it is a purely mechanical and incidental happening. Sex for the sake of sex alone is rather perfunctory and only mildly satisfying. However, if you are a romantic and can summon up even the slightest love for your partner, it is on a sliding scale from ho-hum to magnificent. Although I must admit that to find these things out took more than a little research on my part, however, it was all in the spirit of gentle loving companionship and good, clean fun.

The magnetism existing between male and female is intense in the young and can be both a pleasure and a concern for young couples. I know of nothing that so betrays the good sense of a young man, and I assume a young woman, more than believing one is in love. Sexual attraction and love are difficult to differentiate and more than a few people have fallen into the fatal trap of a marriage with nothing going for it except that they were good in bed. That circumstance does not bode well for a lengthy relationship, married or not.

Sex also has several bad side effects like pregnancy or venereal disease. The first of these prevents many young girls from graduating high school which in itself is a shame but of course something that can be remedied. What can't be remedied is if a child is born. That is a catastrophe. Not only is the young girl obligated much too early to the mothering of a child but the child is handicapped by having a mother that is unready, uneducated and in all likelihood unable to care for an infant.

Don't get me wrong I'm all for sex. I think it's healthy, satisfying, and fun. It is also dangerous because it can lead to pregnancy, mental upset, physical problems (like herpes, or several other unpleasant diseases), and a degradation of self-respect. Sex is one of those double-edged swords in life. It's a lot like handling an explosive—treat it respectfully and it is rewarding; treat it too casually and the results can be devastating.

Day 68.

"To him who in the love of nature holds
Communion with her visible forms, she speaks
A various language.

—W. C. Bryant

❧   ❧   ❧

Except for a general malaise, I feel pretty good. I don't think I have ever totally recovered from my little bout with the flu or ague or whatever the hell it was. I've generally gone downhill health wise since I've been up here and that was something I never counted on. I didn't for a moment think I wasn't healthy enough or strong enough to survive this ordeal. But I can see now that the rain and the cold and the lack of exercise have debilitated me to a great extent. I don't like it.

I think the greatest poet that ever lived was T. S. Eliot and the greatest of his poems is *The Love Song of J. Alfred Prufrock*. I first read that poem along with several others of his when I was a freshman in college. I didn't understand a damn thing about *Prufrock* at that time. I loved the meter and the rhyme and the music in the words but its meaning completely escaped me. Strangely enough it had some kind of hold on me, a fascination, that kept me reading and re-reading it year after year. And, as I re-read it every year more and more of it became clear. It seems as though I had to live more in order to understand more. Now that I am an old man I think I understand it all. It has only taken me 53 years to finally get it.

There are so many wonderful passages in that poem that no one of them truly stands out. Each line is a masterpiece and says so much that it is no wonder it took me all this time to understand. I feel some of those lines so intensely because they are reflections of my own life (maybe they are of everyone's). Lines like:

> "No! I am not Prince Hamlet, nor was meant to be;
> Am an attendant lord, one that will do
> To swell a progress, start a scene or two,
> Advise the Prince, no doubt an easy tool,
> Deferential, glad to be of use,
> Politic, cautious, and meticulous;
> Full of high sentence, but a bit obtuse;
> At times, indeed, almost ridiculous-
> At times, indeed, almost the fool."

Day 69.

"...There will be time, there will be time
To prepare a face to meet the faces that you meet..."

—T. S. Eliot

❧   ❧   ❧

Eliot's poetry questions much of the same things I do. His line about preparing a face to meet the faces that you meet, sends me off thinking about how all of us disguise ourselves in one way or another to meet or avoid some circumstance that we think calls for a particular appearance. We hide behind masks according to what we think the situation requires and part of it is to better serve the person or the crowd we are then associating with, or to hide our fear, anxiety, boredom, or recalcitrance.

We all wear these faces and sometimes it really is who we are, but most times it is simply a subterfuge that hides the real person beneath. I don't have much use for mankind at large. I see it as a faceless mass that is best described by a poem I once read by (I can't remember his first name), Campbell, which, as far as I remember goes:

"When in dead lands,
Where men like brutish herds rush to and fro,
By aimless frenzies borne,
A poet of his own disdain is born,
And dares among the rabble to emerge."

It was so long ago that I read this poem I'm not sure I have it exactly right, but I do remember his disdain for the mass of people populating the Earth, and I'm inclined to agree with him. However, it seems that whenever I get in a one-on-one situation, if the person is not a complete ass, and condescends to let me peek behind the mask he or she is wearing at the time, then all of a sudden you see the human being residing there and you find someone to relate to. Usually, this happens when alcohol is involved for a person is more likely to let a little of themselves show through when their inhibitions are down. And, it is delightful to meet the real person. Often there is more to see in that person than you would expect.

My good friend, Mic, staunchly declares that people are no damned good and he presents a pretty good case for his conclusion. I don't share that opinion except where the mass of people is concerned. However, as I said, in one-on-one, I think I can like almost anyone and see the good in them. The true identity lies behind the mask and to really know a person he or she must be willing to forgo the facade that betrays who they really are.

Day 70.

"A brave man may fall, but cannot yield."

—Dryden

❧   ❧   ❧

I'm still feeling somewhat giddy. I don't think I'm sick but just out of sorts. How else could I feel after spending what feels like my whole life alone, high in a tree, without any human contact except through a bullhorn? I'm really not a suitable companion for myself, I am much too moody, depressed, angry with myself, and homesick for the things I gave up to be a dumbshit. I'll never forgive myself for this. I have the distinction of being very stupid at times, but this takes the cake. If I live long enough to get down to earth again I swear I am going to change the way I am.

However, that's easy to say and almost impossible to do. It's the old story about the scorpion and the frog, where the frog agrees to ferry the scorpion across the river if he promises not to sting him. And, of course, in mid-stream the scorpion stings him and when the frog asks him why, because now they both will drown, the scorpion answers, "I couldn't help it. It's my nature."

I'll probably be the same way. In time I will forget this experience and revert to my true nature, whatever that is. I have the feeling it's not too nice.

My brother was a hero. He was always a hero to me because he was 13 years older, better looking, had all the pretty girls in town chasing after him, became a pilot in WWII, and had to be the best looking guy in the Air Force. Anyway, he was indeed a hero, he was awarded the Bronze Star in the Korean War, for helping evacuate the 1st Marine Division out of the enemy encirclement at the Chosin Reservoir. He and several other pilots flew into the heart of the action and got the marines out of where they were sure to be exterminated. Damn his hide he got the chance to be a hero. I never did and that has caused me severe distress throughout my life. You see, I would like to have been him. He had all the adventure and I had the leavings. I don't resent him having all that adventure. I just resent my having none.

Like all wild things,
My dreams rejoice in being wild.

They soar on Eagle's wings,
And treat with Gods,
And pay no heed
To humdrum deeds below.

Day 71.

"…gone too soon, like our youth, away."

—Irish Folk song

❋   ❋   ❋

I just remembered my first attempt at writing and publishing when I was about seven or eight. I started by laboriously typing "The Bulletin," on our old Royal typewriter complete with mistakes, erasures, and spelling errors. It was my first attempt in the world of literature.

"The Bulletin" was a one page neighborhood newspaper that mainly reflected my personal observations of the seasons, any significant events which might affect the neighborhood (not many of those), announcements of up-coming school activities such as the sale of Christmas Seals or sports days, and a liberal plagiary of poetry or short inspirational clips from the local newspaper or the magazines of the time.

When I completed each issue I attempted to peddle my "newspaper" to our neighbors who good-naturedly paid the price of five cents a copy. I think there were only three editions before I turned my attention to some other get-rich-quick scheme. I wrote an article about Butch in "The Bulletin," a copy of which, in the good care of my mother, survived the punishment of the years. Upon review, these many years later, I found the article which ended with a poem from some unknown source that had found its way into the book where I kept my grandfather's poems. If I can remember, It goes like this:

<u>CHUMS</u>

He sits and begs, he gives a paw,
He is, as you can see,
The finest dog you ever saw
And he belongs to me.

He follows everywhere I go
And even when I swim.
I laugh because he thinks, you know,
That I belong to him.

But still no matter what we do
We never have a fuss,
And so I guess it must be true
That we belong to us.

—Anonymous

Sometimes my father, Butch and I would go down to the river to fish. My father would buy a pound of liver for bait if we had failed to dig worms in preparation. Of all things in this world Butch loved liver best so when we were at the river I would bait my hook and cut a small piece for Butch and he would wait patiently until either Dad or myself had to bait our hooks again when, he knew, he would get another bite.

One day Dad and I decided rather late that we would go to the river to see if the fish were biting. We stopped at the market and Dad bought the liver, and we went to our fishing spot and baited our hooks. Butch, of course got his tidbit.

We sat for some time and the evening was deepening, the sun setting low on the horizon, when we pulled our lines in and saw that our bait was gone, I turned to get the liver which we had left wrapped in the butcher paper, and there sat Butch wagging his tail in an extremely agitated manner, looking, as only he could, obsequiously apologetic and pleading with his eyes as if to say "I couldn't help myself." The pound of liver was gone and a small piece of the paper clung to the side of Butch's mouth.

Instead of being terribly upset my father laughed and we pulled Butch in between us. The three of us sat watching the river roll past, as the pleasant evening surrounded us in a cloak of amber.

Late on a Summer's afternoon
We'd fish down on the river
Till after sundown.

The two of us would sit
With the dog close in between,
Not far from water's edge
And intently listen
To the quiet world
The river knew.

There along the river's twisting way
We watched the water roll
In easy and unending flow,
Muddy brown
Screened through the Summer's haze.

Born from gently weeping snows
In our high mountains
Which rose in stoic majesty
To tease the drifting clouds
And slow the hasty desert wind.

Here now at our feet
The giant brown carpet of its waters
Moves in august silence
From out its high proud past beginnings
To some secret rendezvous.

Day 72.

"Know thou this:—that men
Are as the time is."

—Shakespeare

❦   ❦   ❦

Thinking about Dad and Butch sent me off thinking about my father. He was a good man.

I really got to know my Dad when he and I worked together. He was a hard worker, honest, never complained, just took things as they came, as I said, he was courageous. A real man. One I could admire, participate with, and love deeply.

He was also the one who taught me what it was to be a man. My rite-of-passage was when I was old enough to go on the deer hunts with the men in my family and their friends. It was there that he taught me discipline.

First there was the discipline of the gun. I learned that before I ever went hunting. We always had a lot of guns in the house, never loaded, but when we went target shooting I learned that a gun is always pointed at the sky or at the ground when you're not shooting. You never carried a gun with a cartridge in the chamber. You never shot anything unless you were reasonably sure of a kill and if you only wounded an animal you tracked it until you found it and made sure it was dead.

Then there was the discipline of the hunt: You never, but never, complained; you always helped with all the work; you never showed fear or any emotion that could be attributed to the female gender such as crying; and if there was any hard or very disagreeable job to be done you always stepped forward. It was a tough training camp and I loved it.

Mom and Dad were funny about me in some ways. Neither one of them attended my graduation from high school or from college. I don't know why exactly but I had the distinct feeling that they felt I was going beyond them, in some way leaving them, and maybe looking down on them. God knows I never did that. I admired them both more than anyone else in the world. Maybe I never told them and I'm sorry for that.

They also never gave me any sex education. Sex was never mentioned in our house and I was left to find out about it by my own devices. In addition, any consideration of a career was never brought up. I was pretty much left to figure out my future by myself. I never knew anything about scholarships or colleges other than the junior college in my hometown. I had not the slightest idea of what opportunities existed outside my little town and so I went into the world with very little support and no guidance at all. I guess it was just the way they had gone into the world, and they probably thought that was just the way it was done.

Day 73.

"…when old midnight comes around."

❧　　　❧　　　❧

I don't think I'd make a very good crook. It's not that I'm too honest, it's just that I probably wouldn't be bright enough and I'd be too clumsy. Believe it or not I have dreamed about stealing something that I really covet. It's a sculpture and probably weighs about a thousand pounds. It wouldn't be an easy heist.

When my grandfather was homesteading in Oklahoma Territory he had a pair of matched mules. Their names were Maude and Myrtle. They must have been splendid animals because my grandfather loved them dearly.

My grandmother was Scotch-Irish, meaning she was a protestant, an Orangeman or, rather, an Orange person. However, being Irish she had a magnificent temper and when she brought it to the surface my grandfather and their seven sons would head for the tall timber. When it was directed toward my grandfather he would go out and hitch up Maude and Myrtle and plow the fields, sometimes all night.

Anyway, I've fallen in love with this sculpture. It is of a pair of horses, their heads really. They are workhorses in full harness and the definition of the horses and the intricate detail of their harness is incredible. One is nuzzling the other with his huge head and the expression in both of them is as if they were in a field pulling a plow and doing their work. It is so real it makes you weep. Their names are Maude and Lottie. Close enough to Maude and Myrtle, even if they aren't mules.

The sculpture is in a park of sculptures, all magnificent, and this particular one is by a well-known animal sculptor by the name of Cammie Lundeen. The horse's heads are mounted on a giant block of marble which would also contribute to the difficulty of stealing them.

I love that sculpture so much that I have imagined going to the park in the middle of the night with the biggest heavy lift machine I could find and physically removing it. Then what would I do? Where could I hide something that measures six or seven foot tall by four foot square and weighs, with the marble block, at least a ton. I could hardly put it in my backyard. It would be a little obvious to the neighbors. I couldn't get it in the house and if I could the floor joists probably couldn't support it and it would end up in my basement. It's a quandary that I'm working on.

I wonder what the sentence would be for stealing a sculpture? Like I said I don't think I would be a very good crook.

Day 74.

"The resultant of forces acting upon the boundaries of any arbitrary region, is equal to the summation of the time rate of change of the bodies or particles within that region."

—Unknown

❧   ❧   ❧

I had to put down that quote just to see if I could remember it. It is a wonderfully verbose statement for "Every action has an equal and opposite reaction." However, my reason for using it was just to make sure I wasn't losing my mind.

Day after day I question my sanity. First of all for engaging in this imbecilic scheme, and secondly, I wonder if I'm losing my mind. I have been thinking and reminiscing and theorizing and speculating so much that I feel like the little boy with one shoe nailed to the floor, just going around in circles. I never questioned my sanity before so this is a brand new experience. One I would just as soon forego.

It makes you wonder just what sanity is anyway. Is everybody sane? Except, of course, for those who obviously aren't. But is there a big difference. I think I remember one of my professors saying, that insanity is only a matter of degree. I assumed he meant that we're all a little insane it's just that some of us are more insane than others. I can go along with that.

I had an aunt that I swear would go a little nuts when the moon was full. And, I guess from police statistics and hospital records that the full moon does affect some people strangely. Be that as it may, I have always regarded myself as completely, totally, sane, although I must admit that I've done some pretty bizarre things in my life. But is bizarre, insane? I guess it could be. It would just depend on how much over the edge you were.

I think a lot of people are troubled. I was walking to the cafeteria one day with one of my coworkers when he reached into his pocket and pulled out four 357-magnum bullets. He held them in his open hand and said to me, "There's a name on each one of them." I chuckled nervously and looked at him to see if he was joking but he was "deadly" serious. I half-heartedly said "Well, I hope my name isn't on one of them." He said, "No, but they know who they are. They're trying to steal my invention."

"Oh," I said, "what invention is that?"

"You don't want to know." He said.

"You're right," I said.

Well I mentioned it to a security guard as soon as I could find one, and before the afternoon was out my companion was being escorted to the local booby hatch. I never saw him again and I was glad about that.

So I would say he was over the edge but what of all these other folks out there that do weird things. My God, weird is all over the place. Go to a high school "Kegger," sometime or a wingding of a party that teenagers or twenty-somethings are throwing. They're pretty way out. And, how about "road rage," and drive-by shootings? Are they acts of sanity? I think that a lot of what we call crime is really insanity. Murder for example. How sane is a person who plans and executes the murder of someone? That's not rational behavior. For that matter, how about "Picket's Charge" or the "Charge of the Light Brigade" or the French Revolution, where any and all of the learned people of the country were killed simply to satisfy the blood lust of the mob? Isn't that all insanity?

For that matter, isn't all mob violence insanity? Maybe I have been looking for the reason why we are so good at killing one another in all the wrong places. Just maybe it's our insanity acting out. Maybe at heart man so dislikes his fellow man that given the opportunity to give way to our innate insanity we gleefully destroy each other.

And there is another aspect of that theory. I have long believed that our "fear" of death is really not a "fear" at all. Rather it is a love of death brought about by its inevitability, our own and everyone else's. We don't really fear death, we fear its trappings: illness, pain, suffering, and diminished life. We fear the prospect of death far more than death itself. The greatest ingredient in this love of death is that we really don't revere life all that much. Life is hard. It is struggle, and pain, and anxiety, and suffering, and loss, and fear, and boredom, and waiting, and, and, and. It has its moments of joy but they are few and far between, otherwise it is a slow, grinding, and debilitating process of dying. Why wouldn't death be attractive. At the end of one's life "to shuffle off this mortal coil" becomes more and more desirable to the point where not only is one ready to die, it becomes their most devout wish.

So do we really believe that depriving someone of life is such a grievous offence? Not if one is miserable in their own life. Indeed, they may think that the person's life was not worth living in the first place. They may think that everyone will be better off in paradise or heaven or oblivion. We wouldn't have to pack around this heavy, aching body for one thing, and we could dump all of our peculiar sorrows and afflictions and leave this world of cares and woes and maybe end up the better for it.

Am I nuts? Endorsing death would make me seem so. And, perhaps, just perhaps, I'm a little to the left of center on the scale of the insane but that would just make me eccentric—not bonkers.

Day 75.

"The paths of glory lead but to the grave."

—Gray's Elegy

✿   ✿   ✿

I was just thinking back to one day in the Supermarket a couple weeks before I came up here. At the time it was a very unpleasant experience but I think I see it differently now.

I was standing in a checkout line at the grocery store cursing my inevitable luck for finding the line where the clerk and the customers are having the most problems, where the first customer in line, an express line with a sign that clearly stated "MAXIMUM OF SIX ITEMS ONLY—CASH ONLY", was positioning a minimum of 15 items on the conveyor belt. My agitation grew as each item was rung up and the customer, a gray-haired and argumentative old lady, who was obviously mentally disadvantaged, saw fit to challenge the price on several items, and then struggled to find the exact change, down to the last penny, in a totally inadequate coin purse into which she hopelessly thrust her pudgy hands to retrieve that last elusive cent.

Finally, to the great relief of those of us behind her, she was paid, her groceries bagged, and loaded into a cart for the trek to her car where she would undoubtedly frustrate several more passersby as she loaded her purchases into the car, and backed haphazardly into the oncoming traffic to make her exit.

To make matters worse, the gentleman in front of me, apparently unfamiliar with the word "CASH," retrieved his checkbook from his rear pocket and proceeded to consume several of my precious minutes by laboriously filling out a check for three dollars and eleven cents. Whereupon the clerk then had to see his driver's license, copy down the number, run it through a check checking machine, place it in the tray beneath the cash drawer, wait for the automatic receipt typing machine to provide a receipt while she bagged his four items, gave him the receipt and wished him a nice day.

All this time the knot in my stomach had tightened to the point of nausea and I'm sure that the vibrations I was giving off would have offended Attila the Hun. I paid for my one purchase, with CASH, waived the offer of a sack, thanked the clerk, and proceeded to grumble at the stupidity of people all the way to the car.

Usually I forget such incidents as quickly as they happen but I recalled this one immediately after reading an account of the siege of Leningrad in the winter of 1941–42 in Alexander Werth's book, *Russia At War, 1941–1945.*

Mr. Werth gave a startlingly clear account of what conditions and food supplies were like for the people of Leningrad. As I recall he said that the populace lived on 1,000 or less calories per day and that was an optimistic exaggeration. Meat and fats were replaced by substitutes like sheep-guts jelly. Oh, my God!

I think I remember him saying that in one month, December 1941, over 50,000 people died, as many as normally died in a year and in the first months of 1942, between 3,500 and 4,000 people died every day. During the early stages of the blockade, he estimated that 900,000 people had died, and if my memory serves me, I have seen even higher figures than that.

People suffered and died from hunger, and the terrible cold in unheated houses. To try to find something to eat they would try to catch crows or rooks, or any cat or dog that had still somehow survived; they would go through medicine chests in search of castor oil, hair oil, Vaseline or glycerin; they would make soup or jelly out of carpenter's glue (scraped off wallpaper or broken-up furniture). People died everywhere, in the streets, their houses, or at their work in factories.

The dead bodies would usually be put on a hand-sleigh drawn by two or three members of the dead man's family; but often these exhausted family members would be forced to abandon the body halfway to the cemetery.

Remembering these words I thought back to my impatience while waiting in a line in a magnificent store filled to overflowing with food of all kinds. Food from all over the country and, indeed, the world. Food, enough in that store, to have fed most of the people of Leningrad, at least something, for many days. I marveled at how very small, selfish and petty I have grown.

Here I am in this blessed land of plenty, filling my grocery cart and my belly with any food of my heart's desire and all I find to do is curse the length of time it takes me to get through the checkout line.

How sad it is that we cannot constantly bring history with us in our minds, to remind us how fortunate we are. Maybe, just maybe, if we could remember the struggles of others, even our own forebears, we could reduce our impatience, our anxieties, and sometimes, our rage, at those things or people who interfere with our perception of what we think ought to be. A little comparison of our lives versus that of others might make us better than we are.

Day 76.

"The inaudible and noiseless foot of time."

—Shakespeare

❦   ❦   ❦

Hallelujah! Only 25 more agonizing days to go. I should rejoice but 25 days seems like a lifetime. Isn't it strange how time is distorted according to whether it is in front of you or behind you? Take the phrase "Twenty years from now," compared with "Twenty years ago." The first seems like it is forever in the future and the latter seems like only yesterday. Right now, to me, 25 days seems a terribly long way off.

Time is deceitful. It is an intriguing subject. You can say so many things about it and yet it remains illusive. Let's face it, time is a human construct, based on our position with regard to our sun. And, if you consider that our sun is a "dwarf G-zero star," three quarters of the way out on one of the spiral arms of the galaxy we call "the Milky Way," our time doesn't seem all that factual or important. Of course, it is to us.

It regulates practically everything we do in our brief lifetimes. We get born at a certain time which we then celebrate every year, "at the same time." We plan our days and our appointments, our comings and goings, our careers, our liaisons, our meals, our sleep, all by the clocks we have invented to guide our way through time. We plant our crops, and harvest them; yearly we see the new cars arrive on the scene; we count our births and deaths, and all the goings on in between by our small and universally insignificant time calculations.

Back when most of the people of the world were farmers of one sort or another, we lived by a different time, a natural time, dictated by the rising and setting of our sun. However, since becoming an urban society we have changed from natural time to one of accelerated demand where time is dictated by the exigency of the moment. Now with the advent of computers and ultra fast computer games the young people exist in an infinitely quicker time where seconds are the measure of events and minutes seem like an eternity.

Thinking on this, I felt inspired enough to overcome my malaise and develop a poem. Not a very good one I'm afraid, but then, what the hell, I'm sick.

Time wears many faces,

The deeper rut the river wears,

The moss that crawls along the wall,

The circle deep within the eyes

Of ancient men,

The halting footsteps

Of the bearers of the pall.

Deeply time engraves its traces,

Marks upon us all its ceaseless change,

Prepares the earth to receive us,

Then melts the headstone

Marking out our graves.

Day 77.

"If you're not here now,
You're not anywhere."

—Ram Dass

❦　　　❦　　　❦

My wife is into a lot of self-help books by various authors. I read some of them but don't find anything that I don't already know. The biggest theme seems to be, "Be Here Now." Well, I read a book by that name by Ram Dass back in the 1960's. It was a wonderful book and I kept it and studied it for years.

All of these books make the point that we can't live in the past and sure as hell can't live in the future so our only option is to be here now. Seems pretty obvious and yet there are people, and maybe I'm one of them, who spend a lot of their time in the past. Moreover, there are the other types that concern themselves more with the future than they do with the present.

The real message is that if we don't live the present moment we are wasting our precious time. You've got to be aware of the now, the things around you, the pleasure and beauty of what you see, the realization of what is going on at this moment inside and out. Make every action important, see it for what it is, and delight in your presence here.

I sure subscribe to that although at the present time, there's not a hell of a lot going on in this tree. Oh, there are a few birds quarreling, what about, I haven't the slightest idea, but that's about the size of it. So I'm inside my head and it is very difficult to "be here now" with what's in my consciousness.

As I have said, with nothing going on up here, and being unable to foretell the future, what can I do but look backward or speculate about things I don't know answers to. So, what's a fellow to do. I'm caught in a trap of my own design and for the next 24 days I can only do what I've been doing, and eagerly look forward to when I'm back to my life and can really appreciate "being here now."

If I could distill each day
Down to its essence,
And throw away
All that is not real,
How much of what
Would I contain,
What quantity,
What substance,
Would remain?

Day 78.

"Cannery Row in Monterey in California is a poem, a stink, a grating noise…"

—Steinbeck

❦   ❦   ❦

I first went to California in 1951 and thought I had landed in paradise. It was a lovely place at that time before it was discovered by half the country and people by the millions crowded in. I lived in the small beach town of Redondo Beach and it had a fishing pier, an old one, where you could walk down a row of fish vendors and buy all kinds of fish, shellfish, smoked fish and even a hamburger if you were crazy. I used to spend an afternoon on that pier eating smoked Bonita and drinking a German beer.

Redondo Beach was right next door to Hermosa Beach and a club called the Lighthouse where some of the great jazz artists of all time played nightly. I thought I was as close to heaven as I had ever been.

L. A. was a strange and wonderful place. I would go down to Wiltshire Boulevard on a Saturday or Sunday and just walk the streets marveling at all the shops and the general ambience of the place. It was a real thrill to me, coming from such a small town, to be in a metropolis, to feel the energy and the dynamism of the place but it always made me feel inadequate, as though I wasn't of the character needed to succeed in such a place.

My fascination with L. A. continued for a long time and I would go sometimes early in the morning, on a Sunday, to see it quiet and asleep. It had a melancholy feeling to it then, and I was struck with the fact that without people it was all just concrete and steel, derelict, lifeless.

I have roamed the alien world
Of deserted, wind-blown streets,
On lonely Sunday mornings
Within the empty city.

I have visited the wasteland,
Wherein forsaken buildings stand
Sternly quiet, as ancient derelicts,
In timeless gloom.

I have seen the useless remnants,
Cluttered asphalt,
Silent steel,
Impassive concrete,
Decaying in sterile sunlight,
Lifeless,
Without beauty,
Alone,
Without purpose.

I was very lonely in California. I was a fish out of water. It was all so new and alien to me. It took me a long time to feel at home. Looking back on it now, I don't think I ever felt at home there. I longed for my mountain bowl and the small town life I had left and I remember wanting to go back so badly, but there was no work to go back to, so I stayed, and continued my loneliness.

Here in this blank dream
Of dying rivers and bitter dust
Souls shrink and spirits whither.

Petty histories consume the present,
And our lives scurry past our view
Like dusty rodents seeking refuge
From the air and sunlight.

Day 79.

"A day without sunshine
Is like a day without Sarsaparilla."

—Anon

❧   ❧   ❧

The weather has turned out beautiful. Sunshine, blessed sunshine is painting the landscape with gold and warmth. It has lightened my heart.

Twenty days to go. Oh, brother, will this unendurable trial never end? I do so miss my wife, the comfort of her arms, her sweet disposition, her generous nature. I got lucky when I found her.

Marriage is a funny thing, maybe funny is the wrong word, curious is better. Anyway, marriage is at once wonderful, and comfortable, and spiritually elevating, and confining, and restrictive, and unsettling. It is a confusion of emotional states that both male and female encompass. Men are more likely to resent the restraint on their freedom and women are more likely to dislike the obligations her husband represents. However, both of them reap many benefits, otherwise, they would make short work of their marriage in a divorce court.

I read *Men are from Mars; Women are from Venus*, when it first came out and I must say that book was a work of art. Until I read that book I thought I must be the original "son-of-a-bitch" because of the way I acted toward women and especially my wife. Then I read that all men act the way I do and I'm really not such a bad guy after all.

Reading about women gave me insights I wish I had received when I was a young man. It would have clarified so much about women that I never did understand. What it amounts to is that we all need a course early on studying the differences between the sexes so that we don't stub our toes when trying to get along.

It gave me a brand new appreciation for women and, like I say, it liberated me from the idea that I was different from all other men in what I thought, and the way I acted. Dr. John Gray performed a real service to mankind.

Day 80.

"...seek introductions, favors, influences? No thank you..."

—Rostand

❧   ❧   ❧

Fame. Why would anyone ever want fame? Oh, I imagine it is a great ego builder but I, for one, do not need any more ego construction. I have quite enough as it is. However, it seems that there are a lot of people pursuing fame. It must be some kind of a head-trip but I think it would have some seriously deleterious effects on one's personality. I look at all the so-called celebrities and I don't think I like them. I might like one or two individually but most of them appear to be superficial, and so totally self-absorbed that it would be difficult to get their attention.

I went to lunch in Hollywood once with a would-be celebrity. He had starred in a couple of successful movies but he was far from being classified as a "Star." Anyway, we went to the Brown Derby where I had a Cobb Salad, (supposedly from the original recipe), and he had something he didn't have to eat so that he could spend his time looking for someone to impress. We had very little conversation. I don't think he even looked at me through the entire meal. I'm sure he must have had a strained neck muscle from all of his rubbernecking around the place. It was not a pleasant luncheon but, at least, I let him pay the tab.

For a time I was associated with some Hollywood types and by and large it all was regrettable. Most of the people I knew were "aspiring," not really recognized actors or actresses at all, and these are the worst of the Hollywooders.

They are so focused on their attempts to become known that it brought out their very worst qualities. They are willing to do anything to get their names in lights or even on a poster or in the list of credits, in extremely small letters. They are truly fame-seekers and they are pathetic.

I read about the so-called Rock Stars and see them on TV with their immense entourage of would-also-bes and I wonder what a life like that would be. I can't imagine all the chaos surrounding them all the time, not to mention during their performances. I wouldn't like having to shout nonsensical sounds into a sputum-laden, phallic-shaped microphone while a throng of music-maddened adolescents screamed and fainted and threw-up over one another.

Maybe I'm just too old to appreciate that kind of thing.

However, they aren't the only ones getting this outrageous attention. Look at Princess Diana or TV personalities or sports figures, they all have their fans chasing after them, not to mention the paparazzi. What a hell of a life, being chased by mindless curiosity-seekers or signature collectors or photo hounds, twenty-four hours a day.

Not my idea of a good life.

Speaking of the good life, I can't really claim that I've been living one for the past couple of months or so. The so-called "good life" is a really simple thing, I think. It consists of three things that I must attribute to an old Chinese proverb. It goes like this: "The three essentials of happiness are: something to do; something to love; and something to hope for." Pretty simple, huh? And, if you analyze it what else is there?

The something to do can be anything, your life's work, your hobby, your creative expressions, even your mundane day-to-day job (if you enjoy it or take pride in it or even just see it as your means to live).

Something to love includes your mate, your family, your friends, even those you socialize with, if you can enjoy their company. It also may include animals, nature, leisure time enjoyments, or the pursuit of your passion such as writing, or painting, or music.

Something to hope for can include anything your heart desires. All of the things that represent to us the fulfillment of life from accomplishment to self-actualization, to being able to say at the end that you have lived a good life.

Within those three personal principles a life can be whatever one wants to make it. I've come to realize that those are the things that make life worthwhile and without any one of them life can be at the least—wanting, at the most—empty.

Right now I am wanting all three; something to do, besides sit in an empty, dark dungeon of my own design; something to love, and I'd like that something to be with me if you please; and my ardent hope is that I survive this idiot scheme of mine without losing my mind. It seems I'm good at hoping, I will write a poem about it.

My fickle nature now
Is longing for flowers
And the budding trees.

Not long ago
I wished for snow,
Then, in Summer,
The Fall with dying leaves.

When young,
I embraced the constant change,
And sighed relief,
At having something new to do.

But now my age
Has made me timorous,
I cannot chance the change
My whole heart longs for,
And fear
Usurps my eagerness.

Day 81.

"...I only know a man ain't got a friend,
Without a song."

❧   ❧   ❧

Twenty more days to go. I think my tank is on empty, both physically and mentally. Emotionally I passed the empty mark many, many days ago. I now feel kind of numb but still appalled at my stupidity. What I am most appalled about is realizing all the things that I have started neglecting over the years. Things like family, my lovely wife, my children, my friends. I guess I was in the process of becoming a rancorous old hermit even in the midst of those who love me and who are most concerned for my welfare.

I wanted free time, to be alone, to be self-centered and self-occupied, to write and indulge myself in my fantasies and my memories. Somehow I lost track of how important the family and social contacts really were to me and moreover, I forgot how to be civil to the people I interacted with daily. I became so self-centered that I denied my attention, my concern, and my demonstrable love for those around me. I had hit bottom on the scale of my social ability.

I was becoming irascible and cantankerous. An old man, with a nasty disposition. I don't want to be that way. I want to enjoy all aspects of my life, what little there is left of it, and a big part of that life has to be the socialization that I have so avoided in the past.

One-on-one I generally like people, especially if they will let their hair down and be real for a time. My wife is wonderful at getting people to remove their masks and expose the real person they are. She is so honest and forthright that people trust her with their feelings and their private thoughts. She gets back what she gives out and it is a great contribution to all those around her.

On the other hand I find it slow going to get to know another person and being a typical man I can't discuss my personal feelings or delve into another man's thoughts and emotions. Men just don't do that sort of thing. So all my contact with men is on a superficial level except for one or two very special friends with whom I can share my thoughts and beliefs. Even then it is usually guarded because I value their friendship so much that I don't want to alienate them in any way.

Getting back to my growing callousness over the years towards those people I really care for, I want to change my direction when I descend from this high hell. I want to become a better man and I want to show everyone how I feel about them, how I value them, and how I want them to participate in my life just as I wish to participate in theirs. I think I *will* change because this experience in the tree has caused me to reevaluate many things that are precious to me, but that I was well on my way to abrogating.

Now at evening
The day can be assessed,
The giant swing of sun,
The endless shifting of the light,
The tides of faces moving fast,
The beginning and the last
Of each moment's hurried glance,
Of the passing and the past.

Day 82.

"Humor is the poor man's riches."

—Anon

❀   ❀   ❀

It seems my thoughts and the writings in my journal have been very heavy lately. I'm not talking to Charlie anymore and, let's face it, I'm depressed and lonely and still not feeling well. It's hard to overcome this malaise I seem to be drowning in but I keep swimming. I'm going to recall some of the funny stories and incidents that I remember and maybe that will elevate my mood.

Another of my good friends, Bob Weiner, and I worked together as writing consultants for one of the big aircraft proposals in the mid-sixties. Bob was a very funny guy and he and I hit it off from the time we met. We had our desks placed side-by-side and between coffee and cigarettes we would work as many as 50 to 55 hours straight before taking an eight-hour break. Then we would go back to work. We had very tight deadlines and this meant working literally as many hours as we could before we'd drop. I think our record was 113 hours in one week.

Naturally, working those kinds of hours our productivity dropped very low indeed but we did manage to crank the stuff out, and if I remember correctly it wasn't bad.

Bob was Jewish and after our stint on that proposal was over he had me over for a Seder at his house. I had never been to one before so I was duly impressed with the solemnity and the joy in which the whole family participated. I never had studied Judaism much before that but going to that Seder awakened my interest and I started reading about the history of the Jews and about Jewish religion. It was an interesting study although I'm not sure I understand any more about Jews than I do about Christians. Of course they are very closely allied down to the advent of Christ himself and, oh my, there the cleavage began and it took almost two thousand years for them to accept one another and then only conditionally and in some countries. I don't understand religion for this very basic reason: they all teach love and forbearance for one's neighbors but there are more wars fought over religion down through the ages than for any other reason.

I guess I'm just a pagan at heart. I want to go my own way, choose my own god, and practice my own philosophy. That's not asking too much, is it?

Bob was a great storyteller and there is one story that I'm going to write down so I don't forget it. That's a big problem as one gets older. Pretty soon you don't remember even the good times or the good stories.

Anyway, Bob was attached to a Nike anti-aircraft squadron during his military service and his particular group was a mixed bag of characters, like any outfit in the Army.

The sergeant in charge was a grizzled old guy left over from WWII, and was a very strict disciplinarian. For some reason he was especially against vulgar swearing. I guess he'd been around it too much during his career. Therefore, he prohibited his men from ever using swearwords around him especially those with a sexual connotation. However, he had one phrase that was so offensive to him that he threatened corporal punishment to any of his men he heard using it. It was: "Motherfucker."

Of course, being in an anti-aircraft group their training included a lot of aircraft coordination and communication, and an intense discipline to avoid shooting some poor Cessna pilot out of the air. With regard to communication they were instructed never to use the word "Roger," which means, "I understand," or "Wilco," which means "I will comply." The reason for this was because this is pilot talk and having the ground crews using the same words would only lead to confusion.

One day the commanding General made a surprise inspection tour of all the Nike groups in the squadron and to test their readiness and training he would talk to the men lined up before him, asking them questions, ranging from, "How's the food?" to "How do you respond to a plane that does not have IFF (Identification—Friend or Foe) equipment on board?

The General got to a man standing next to my friend Bob, a man who, according to Bob, was not too bright in the first place, and who was terribly nervous at having a General in front of him. The General looked into the man's

Day 83.

"For in religion as in friendship, they who profess most are ever the least sincere."

—Sheridan

❧   ❧   ❧

I had a friend once who was a good Catholic. He was also a very well educated and intelligent guy. He had received his B.A. degree from Loyola University in Los Angeles, and he and I had some rousing conversations about religion in general and Catholicism in particular.

My objections to Catholicism, I told him at the time, was that it seemed to me to be a religion of convenience, in that people could do whatever they damn well pleased and be absolved of any responsibility for their actions. And, that it also seemed to me to be like every other Christian religion as far as the fundamentals were concerned only the "Church" had a long and brutal history of oppression against people who went against the wishes or dogma of the priests, bishops, cardinals, and the pope.

He countered my arguments with his well thought out responses, none of which deterred me from my position. However, in the course of our discussions I did sense the deep respect he had for his religion, and I appreciated the extent of his examination of his beliefs. He had arrived at his concepts independently through much analysis of the basic tenets which he endorsed.

He had studied theology under the guidance of Senior Jesuits at Loyola University and had come away with an education in that subject that the most ardent student of religion would admire. He appeared to me to be a well-schooled believer, who nonetheless admitted that his church had indeed been vile and corrupt at various times in history. He also admitted to the church's culpability in everything from improper behavior by priests to the issuance of Papal Bulls guaranteeing someone's admittance into heaven. He did not excuse the church's history nor its present failings but insisted that the fundamental principles upon which the church had been established were valid.

To me those principles are the same throughout Christendom. I was raised with those principles which stem from the ten commandments, to our basic laws, our basic political system, and our basic social system. And, I don't disagree with them except in practice. Take "Thou shalt not kill," for example. What do we do? We apply a double standard out of necessity, it is: thou shalt not kill except in time of war when it's O.K. Or, how about when Moses came down from the mountain with the tablets carrying the ten commandments and promptly had seventeen thousand Jews executed for worshipping a golden calf. How's that for duplicity?

I have similar concerns about several of the other commandments. By and large the commandments are a good guide to personal behavior. But, then the formation of the commandments into dogma and the obviously self-aggrandizing construction of the Catholic Church in approximately the third century A. D. leaves no doubt in my mind that "the only true church" was blatantly a hoax from the beginning, designed to control the largely ignorant masses of people, extract as much land and money from them as possible, and in return promise them the largesse of the church and its members, and ultimately the bounty of heaven.

I realize these are strong words but to any who doubt my conclusions I would suggest they read the history of the "Church," (one not written by a Catholic), and then study in particular, the crusades, the Inquisition (in Spain and France), and, if one can find books on the subject, the abuses of the priesthood in the dark and middle ages (such as jus primo noctus).

I taught at Loyola University for a brief time, teaching Technical Writing to undergraduate Engineers, who would rather wrestle with the devil than learn to write a complete sentence in English. While there I had contact with several Jesuits and I was always impressed by the extent of their knowledge. I came away with a somewhat strange impression of the few I had contact with. They seemed to me to be extremely intellectual men who put learning actually ahead of religion. I may be wrong in my assessment but they reminded me of the Jews whose study of the Torah became, at least for the moment, the overriding activity in their search for God. The trappings of the church, its matins, its obligatory routines and rituals, its outward appearance to a disinterested public was seemingly secondary, and although all these requirements were assiduously observed by the Jesuits they never appeared to be accomplished with any great zeal or reverence. To me it seemed a perfunctory performance on their part until they could resume their more intellectual pursuits. It was as though the study of the religion was more important than the observation of the religion itself. I could agree with that proposition.

I don't presume to be any great authority on the Catholic Church but I have done considerable study of its history, its power, its wealth, and its control over vast populations. I must admit I do not subscribe to any of its principles or the constructs of its faith. However, as a world power one cannot deny its lofty position.

There is some not-so-nice stuff reported in this country when the flood of Irish Catholics first started in the mid-1800s. A lot of them were destined for the coalmines of Pennsylvania and they were loaded on trains close to the various ports where they docked upon arrival. The trains were then routed to the coalfields but only by routes allowed by the citizenry along the way. For example, no Catholic trains were allowed to enter Philadelphia. All had to be routed around the city.

My grandfather was an avid Catholic hater. He was a Thirty-second degree Mason and as such he disliked Catholics above all others. Something to do with the persecution of the Knights Templars in the twelfth century who then became the Masons. Seems to me that's a long time to carry a grudge. His hatred was restricted to Catholics not to the Irish, because he was married to a native Irish woman, my grandmother, who was Irish, but Scotch-Irish, meaning she was protestant.

At one time I lived in the little village of Cohasset, Massachusetts. While there I learned some of the history of the place and found out that it was founded by protestants who were leaving Boston because of the influx of Catholics. The founders were a strict lot and would not allow any Catholics to settle in the village.

Naturally, there were a few Catholics who resented this exclusion so they went a little distance north of Cohasset and founded the little town of Scituate. But to show they were more tolerant than the citizens of Cohasset they decided they would allow one family of protestants to settle in the town. I don't know if they had any takers or not.

Seems to me this is a wonderful example of the nonsense practiced by these religions and, of course, there are the far more serious and vicious practices

Day 84.

"Take thy correction mildly."

—Shakespeare

❦   ❦   ❦

I once worked for Admiral Charlie Payne, a grand man with a sense of humor. Charlie and I went to dinner one evening and while we were waiting for our dinners to come he related this story to me. It's another one I don't want to forget.

One of Charlie's junior officers told him this true story about when he lived in a neighborhood that was repeatedly the target of Holy Rollers, who would arrive at his home frequently, pushing their views of God upon him, insisting that he take great quantities of printed materials which espoused those views, and asking him to relent and convert to the only true religion (whatever that was).

Over several months it became increasingly intrusive and more than a little ridiculous as they should have realized that there were no converts in that household, nor could they ever expect there to be. But persistent they were. So he decided he would take action against this "...sea of troubles." He went to the local drugstore and bought a small American flag on a six-inch pole stuck in a block of wood, suitable for setting on one's desk.

He put the little flag in the middle of his fireplace mantle and waited. He did not wait long for a few days later there was a knock on his door and when opened there stood a little, somewhat elderly, lady with an armload of advertising material. She said, "Hello, is your wife at home?" "Yes she is," he answered, "won't you come in?"

The little lady stepped inside and said, "I'd like to talk to her a few minutes and to you too, if you have the time."

"Certainly," he said, politely, "but first there is something I would like you to do for me."

"Well, all right," she replied.

Smirking to himself he led her into the living room and up to the mantle, where the little American flag stood all alone.

Knowing that this particular religious sect would not pledge allegiance to any flag or icon because of the first commandment, "Thou shall have no other Gods before me," he smiled patronizingly with satisfaction already thrilling his revenge-filled heart. He said, "Now, would you please say the Pledge of Allegiance to the flag?"

"Well, I guess so," she replied, whereupon she placed her right hand over her heart and rendered an absolutely perfect rendition of the oath.

After completing her assignment, she turned to the now very perplexed master of the house, and said, "I've been an Avon representative for twenty years and that's the first time anyone has ever asked me to do that."

Day 85.

❋ ❋ ❋

I've been thinking a lot about my wife lately and the whole subject of marriage. It seems to me that while marriage itself is a very good thing, we have many stupid expectations from it. It took me three marriages to get it right and there were many reasons that the first two didn't work but that is my point: people change and they change at different rates. One partner may mature while the other simply stagnates at a point in time when it is critical that they both develop their knowledge and personalities at approximately the same rate.

I've witnessed the chasm that appears when a wife decides she wants to be something besides a nursemaid and a house servant. The male response to this behavior is sometimes sufficient to dissolve the marriage. Likewise, the male spouse may become so high and mighty in his workplace that it transfers to his home life with catastrophic results.

People change attitudes, feelings, thought patterns, wishes, desires, goals, and just about everything else incorporated within the human mind. We grow up, grow older, grow old, and these are distinct stages of growth. Each stage has its own requirements and demands, and each has its own limitations.

We seem to be very naive about these changes and limitations however. We don't acknowledge them when we plan our lives and as a consequence we end up paying dearly for our stupidity. But then one usually pays for one's stupidity. I'm a living example of it up here in my tree.

One of the most ridiculous rituals ever invented is the marriage ceremony. First of all it is expensive, ostentatious, and inane. This would be all right if it were not taken so seriously. The wedding vows are almost a guarantee of failure for the couple declaring them. The vows should stop after the first line: "I what's-his-name take thee what's-your-name to be my lawfully wedded spouse." That's enough, don't for heaven's sake go on, because we may all be struck by lightning. The part, "to love, honor, and cherish in sickness and in health," is okay but hard to sustain in difficult times of which, you can be sure, there will be plenty.

It's the last of this oath that is absurd: "for as long as we both shall live." That's crazy. It condemns at least fifty percent of all couples to a condition of breaking what they firmly believe at that time to be a sacred oath.

There is good reason the divorce rate in this country is as high as it is. As I said people change and to commit to a lifelong intimate relationship when most young people are still not quite sure who they themselves are, let alone the person they are marrying, is a hideously stupid thing to do.

Romance is a fickle companion. The young are encumbered by a number of things that shape their ability to reason correctly. Things like lust, dreams, wishes, need for a constant comate, a settled life, a common goal, a surrogate mother, a substitute father, a desire for family, a desire to leave your parent's home and control, etc., etc., etc.

As a temporary fix for these types of things marriage may work but not for long. In a short time the awareness of differences become apparent stripped of the romance which enveloped male and female prior to marriage. When the sexual passion ceases to be a driving factor and sex becomes commonplace whatever else a couple had before marriage is what they are left with. If their interests and goals and levels of maturity are not exceedingly comparable they are in big trouble.

Even if their interests and aims are comparable and the couple is highly compatible, the advent of children in their lives will have an impact on their relationship second only to a nuclear war. Men and women react differently to children especially babies. Thank heavens women have this divinely-endowed "motherly instinct" in caring for the baby otherwise I think the race of man would diminish rapidly and forever. In this circumstance the babies are not the only things that are changed. The allegiances of the man and wife are both altered significantly. More than one husband feels "out in the cold" after a baby is born. His wife's attention is now focused so entirely on the infant that there is little remaining for her husband. It is almost as though the wife had used her male partner to accomplish her end objective—a baby. I realize that this is not necessarily true but somewhere a lurking "perhaps" is hidden in the reasoning of the male, especially when her attention is now so totally elsewhere.

With that out of the way, remember too that, as I have said, people change and the combination of children and growth in different directions can spell the death knell of a marriage.

With all of that relevant and precautionary information just let me finish by saying that marriage with the right partner is a magnificent thing. I highly recommend it.

Day 86.

"Some perversity of mind,
Includes a backward glance,
At closed doors,
And a chapter of life
Read through,
And not to be repeated."

—RRR

❉　　　❉　　　❉

Last year I went to the fiftieth reunion of my high school graduation class. It was amazing to see all those old people gathered together, everybody straining their necks to read the name on the tags hanging on the men's shirts and the women's blouses.

I didn't know anyone so I developed the requisite crick in my neck trying to discern the names on the tags and trying to remember if I ever knew them in high school or out. Of course, I did remember a lot of them and it was good to see them all again. What was not so good was to discover that a full twenty-five percent of my class was already pushing up daisies. That's a pretty high percentage, and among those missing were several good friends. It left me wondering if reunions are pleasant affairs or not. Seeing how much older we all are and reading the obituaries of all those not present was not so damn pleasant because regardless of how you see yourself you know you must look like the rest of them and you're all older than hell.

I don't like thinking of myself that way. To me I'm still a young, swashbuckling cavalier, full of life, capability, and fun. A gay blade with the women, always ready with rapid repartee, adroit, competent, dashing, and, of course, unbelievably handsome. Well, in my dreams. When I have these impressions of myself I dare not approach within twenty feet of a mirror.

I really dislike growing old. It's dispiriting, depressing, discouraging, disheartening, and it hurts. Right now I hurt in virtually every joint in my body, also there is a plethora of muscle aches, and even my hair follicles are painful. I'm not kidding. My hair is bent over to one side because I don't have a suitable pillow (it's a little couch cushion that my wife slipped into the transport basket the last time she sent up food), and, of course, it hasn't been washed in almost three months. Oh, for a good shampoo, a shave, and a haircut. Those mundane things didn't even cross my mind when I decided to come up here. Those little things take on gigantic proportions when you really need them and they are not available.

Back to my reunion. So here we all were surrounded by old people and rubbernecking each other's badge and oh-ing and ah-ing and laughing, and it occurred to me that in probably less than twenty-five years the only thing that would be remaining of the class of '47 would be our pictures in an old annual that somehow had survived all of us. That's all we would be, just pictures in an old book that maybe, just maybe, some kid would glance through one day and marvel at how funny we all looked in our out-dated clothes, our strange hairdo's, and stiffly posed portraits. It will probably give him or her a good laugh before him or her realizes that not too many years hence their picture will appear to a still later reviewer and they will appear as we do now.

Day 87.

"Pride goeth before the fall."

—Bible

✾　　　✾　　　✾

Damn it. I'm getting sick again, This perch is not a healthy environment and I'm feeling bad. Not as bad as I did several or many days ago, can't really remember when it was but I know the symptoms and they're coming back. I'll try to head them off by eating better and getting more rest.

My wife and daughter were back yelling at me through that damnable bull-horn. I sense that my wife is getting very angry and threatens to have my son-in-law come up and force me to go down. But I keep insisting that I'm all right and manage to keep her at bay through imprecations and threats if she persists to bother me. I don't tell her that I'm sick again, of course, she never knew I was sick the other times either.

Now it's a case of having so much time invested in this insane project that I can't give it up, otherwise I would have wasted all my time up here and proved nothing. Actually the only thing I will prove is that I could live a hundred days in a tree. How's that for a significant accomplishment? Right up there with Gandhi or Pasteur, God what a dumb thing to do. I'm sure I'll go down in history for my wonderful contribution to the betterment of mankind. They'll put me in the Guinness Book of Records as the dumbest man for the longest time on record. Additionally, they could award me the Nobel Peace Prize for Stupidity. Even that might be something worthy of note, but probably my triumph will just be ignored. God, I hope so.

There are two powerful temptations among the many available to mankind having to do with status and control. These are greed and power. Greed is something we're all familiar with, we all possess more than we're pleased to admit, but it's a typical human failing, it is a corollary to the "good life," that we all so ardently pursue.

But power is something altogether different. It is strange behavior to say the least but it is a consuming desire to some. I don't know why because along with power comes tremendous responsibility for its exercise.

I have been in managerial positions where I have witnessed power and its concomitant destructiveness. I have promoted people to supervisory or managerial positions and watched them become little Napoleons, wreaking havoc on all those around them. I have seen normal, amicable, and reliable people become tyrannical despots over the poor, innocent people they supervised.

Nothing is as intriguing as the human animal. They change in every situation like a chameleon and it is surprising to witness the Dr. Jekyll and Mr. Hyde personalities that lie very shallowly beneath the surface of those you would least likely suspect. The opportunity to gain either in money or power will provide all the evidence you need to see people in their most primitive, selfish, and virtueless condition. It will go a long way toward convincing you that the majority of people are no damn good.

Day 88.

"The thought,
The deadly thought of solitude."

—Keats

❧   ❧   ❧

Somewhere along the way I determined that the only absolutely absolute statement in the world is that *there is nothing absolute*. Notice I didn't say 'absolutely true' statement, I said 'absolute statement,' for I don't even know if that is a "true" statement. There may be something in the world that is absolute. I just don't know of it.

I'm still feeling lousy but I'm trying to fight this bloody thing whatever it is. Maybe there's a high altitude bug (you know 150 feet high), that attacks stupid people who insist on inconsequential causes at great risk to their physical and mental health. Come to think of it there is a lot of that going around.

If I hadn't chosen to become a freelance technological migrant worker, I might have been a doctor. I admire doctors. They are dedicated people who go through hellish schooling and training, work unnatural and excessive hours, ruin their own health trying to protect that of others, study endlessly to keep up with a profession that is in constant and mercurial change, pay outrageous premiums for malpractice insurance, either get no payment or get shorted by insurance companies that aren't in the least interested in medical care, and who jeopardize their marriage and whatever family life they manage to eke out by the very fact that they feel an obligation to help others. Now there's a profession for you. If you're a total idiot with self-destructive tendencies.

I don't think I am that self-destructive, as to the other indictment in that sentence, well, I'm up here, aren't I.

I once told my mother that I had been thinking of becoming a lawyer, and her response was so dramatic that I immediately abandoned the idea. She said, "Oh son, not a *lawyer!*" She actually had tears in her eyes.

Then at one time I considered becoming a missionary. I was very screwed up emotionally at the time. It sounded like a life of contribution, living in strange places among strange people, and becoming a kindly, beloved, father figure to all the innocents who held beliefs different from my own and my religion. Not long afterward I found many secular diversions that persuaded me that I was not cut out for the path of holiness.

I have since come to regard the entire idea of missionary work as the height of arrogance and moral perfidy. The whole concept is based on the self-serving idea that one religion has the inside track to God and that all others lead only to death, if not hell.

The fact that one ideology is considered superior to another is in itself an arrogant assumption and to assume this under the guise of a benevolent religion is the ultimate hypocrisy. It is the same as my saying to someone that I know better than them. I am right and they are wrong regardless of on what I base this conclusion.

To let people live freely as they will and believe what they will should be the goal of any truly enlightened society, for none of us, absolutely none of us, know which is the "right" path or even if there is any. My motto is live, love, laugh, and be happy, for we all know what happens in the end.

Day 89.

"O that this too, too solid flesh would melt."

—Shakespeare

❈   ❈   ❈

Still no better. I just don't feel well and I can't seem to shake it. I'm headachy and cold most of the time. It still rains a lot but I've gotten so I don't even notice it. I do notice the sunshine, however, when it comes. It is truly beautiful up here but by now I'm so used to it that I have to remember to look at it all and appreciate it. Isn't it strange that when we get so accustomed to our surroundings we fail even to see them, and how can you appreciate something if you're not conscious of it?

I think it was Evelyn Waugh in his book *Island*, where he had loudspeakers all over his fictitious island repeatedly announcing, "Attention, attention, attention." The supposed intention of this message was to keep the populace in constant awareness of their being, and the things around them. Not a bad idea, because it seems most of the time we all are impervious to our surroundings. We become so accustomed to them that we drive somewhere and can't for the life of us remember the drive.

We live in our heads too much. We fail to see what the day is like, what the beauties around us are, what are in the faces that we meet, to see the play of light on water, the geese swimming in little ponds, the birds with vibrant colors visiting our trees.

We walk or jog or bicycle wearing headphones listening to CDs played on pocket size players. We keep our heads down or focused on some image or conversation in our head, or simply listening, and not seeing. What a shame to miss the life around us. It is a goodly part of what makes our life worthwhile.

It was Wordsworth that said,

"The world is too much with us: late and soon,
Getting and spending, we lay waste our powers:
Little we see in nature that is ours;
We have given our hearts away, a sordid boon!"

I take regular walks when I'm at home and I can't say that I do it for aerobic reasons. I amble really, to feel the day, to see what I can see, to admire the life around me. I prefer it that way.

Day 90.

"I feel like one
Who treads alone
Some banquet hall deserted,
Whose lights are fled,
Whose garlands dead,
And all but he departed."

—Thomas Moore

❧   ❧   ❧

I'm really very sick. I just can't seem to get rid of this thing. I think I must be very worn down after being up here so long. It's raining again, or should I say still? And, of course, that doesn't make me feel any better.

I was just thinking of the bulletin board I had at the side of my desk in my room at home. The desk I built when I was in the ninth grade to fit in the dormer window hole in the old house. I kept all sorts of things on my bulletin board. Little snippets of poems and prose that I would clip out of the newspaper or a magazine or a book. It seems funny to me now because at that age I doubt that other boys had such a device to provide them inspiration or guidance or whatever. There were lines like: This is the day the lord hath made…" and "Our greatest glory is not in never falling but in rising every time we fall." And, "Right thought, right speech, right action." And, "To strive, to seek, to find, and not to yield."

I put things on it that I thought would make me a good person as I grew up and give me strength and courage and all the virtues I thought, as a twelve year old, would make me a superior man. I was still religious then and at night I used to pray for the same things.

Although I had trouble going over "fool's hill" as a teenager. I never forgot what was on my bulletin board, but I did quit praying. Eventually, I graduated to more pithy poetry, and literature, which I carried largely in my head since my bulletin board remained where it had first been installed and with all my snippets still on it until I removed them after my mother died. There were still such things as bits of Kahlil Gibran's *The Prophet,* and the "No Thank You" speech from *Cyrano de Bergerac,* and the speech of King Henry V to his troops on Saint Crispin's Day at the battle of Agincourt, and a goodly part of Ecclesiastes, "The race is not to the swift," etc., and poems, a good many poems or pieces of poems.

I guess I've always needed those things to carry with me to shore up my lame and halting faith in myself and the world. I can't remember much of those things now, due I suppose, to my deteriorating memory, but also because they don't mean as much to me now or perhaps because I don't need them as much to supplement my own thinking. I can still quote a lot of those wonderful pieces but one seldom has the occasion.

Those things always propped me up, so to speak, they inspired me, they gave me hope, they filled my mind with positive images, they somehow made sense out of my life when I had trouble finding any reason or purpose in it. I know this, they inspired me to think beyond myself and *that* was a monumental contribution.

Day 91.

"...everyday is a life in miniature."

❀   ❀   ❀

Not much better, maybe some, but I still feel like death warmed over. Being sick is not fun, in fact it is damn debilitating. It leaves you feeling weak and lethargic and without the energy to do much of anything. I have read of African villages where everyone is so sick with one disease of another that they cannot do anything.

It's also interesting to read and think about the part disease has played in world history, the plague, the influenza epidemic, malaria, yellow fever, dengue fever, and all the others. The measles that wiped out the inhabitants of south pacific islands. It's nothing to fool around with. And, now all the new diseases, Ebola, AIDS, new strains of TB, Creutzfeldt Jakob disease, and on, and on. It's as though nature keeps creating new challenges for us. It's a game of: Here's a new one, what are you going to do about it?

It occurred to me that I'm addressing everything as though it was all in the United States or at least in the modernized western world. And, that is a clear distortion of facts. My God, look at Africa. Millions of people dying because of disease and civil war and inadequate knowledge and skills, and the means to develop even a self-sustaining economy, let alone a health care system. These conditions exist elsewhere in the world also, just not to the extremes you can see in Africa.

We in this country live in an Alice's Wonderland when it comes to our comforts and convenience and health care. And, we're not satisfied with it. What must it be like to live in the Congo or Mozambique or Ethiopia? I can't even imagine it.

But, right now I'm busy feeling sorry for myself and I can't do anything for the Africans. I've got to make it through the next nine days and I think that's about all I can handle at the moment.

Day 92.

"Sometimes I wonder why I spend each lonely night dreaming of your smile…"

—Hoagy Carmichael

❧　　　❧　　　❧

I'm still holding my own although I have given serious thought to going down. My illness is serious enough that I don't think I'm going to recover without the aid of antibiotics of some sort. But I'll hang in there for another day or two.

My wife comes everyday to find out how I am. She must sense that I'm not doing too good. Wives are like that. So she comes and bullhorns at me to see if I'm still alive and then she sits with her back against a neighboring Redwood and stays for hours.

She calls to me again before she leaves. It's comforting to know I have her as an emergency rescue if I get to where I feel I really need it.

My wife is a truly good person. She has all of the virtues that I don't. She likes people, she's gregarious, outgoing, an extrovert with her feelings and helpfulness. She's generous with her time, tolerant of our children, and grand-children, doesn't swear or use objectionable words most of the time, and, in short, is a genuine, sensitive, sincere, and wholly good person. I, on the other hand, am a shit.

But, what the hell, it takes all kinds to make a world, and where would we be if we were all like my wife? It would be a nice place to live but…boring. We need variety in our lives. When I was a young man I needed a variety of young women, a variety of adventures, a variety of experiences. That's what life is all about, isn't it? Frankly I don't know what life is all about, but variety is certainly a nice part of it.

Speaking of variety, I sure as hell miss it. This experience in the tree has not been exactly exciting. The only thing I have managed to do is dredge up a lot of memories, stir up a lot of speculative introspections, weave a lot of insights and outsights together into a series of questions, and, get sick and feel sorry for myself. What a fun time!

But then if I hadn't been doing this what else would I have done. Probably accomplished some dull and meaningless writing in my study, gone for my walks, eaten good home cooked hot meals, slept in a soft comfortable bed, lazed around our comfy home, taking naps, reading, visiting with my wife. Oh God, I may cry!

Before I came up here it seemed like a too quiet, boring life. Now I wouldn't trade it for anything in the world. Why, in heaven's name did I ever think I was tired of it all?

I remember standing in the rain,
Atop a broad flat mountain,
Listening to the music
Of rain, and wind in pine trees,
And feeling clouds
With cold wet faces,
And yielding earth,
The flash of electric fire,
And the roll of thunder-drums,
Through mountain valleys,
And I was Adam in Eden,
With earth and heaven and God.

Day 93.

"Darn that dream I dreamed last night…"

—Song—Darn That Dream

❦　　　❦　　　❦

Still sick. I feel better in the mornings but by noon I'm beginning to fade and by evening I feel like I'm dying. But then a night's sleep puts me back on my feet.

This morning I was recalling some of the old songs that I grew up with and some of them even into the sixties. Whatever happened to sentimentality? I think somewhere along the way it became a dirty word. I didn't particularly like all of the old love songs but there were some great ones and they expressed a gentleness that I don't see much of in our society anymore. I wonder if it has been bred out of us.

The kids these days don't seem to cater to gentleness much. They appear somewhat hard and cynical. Their music sure reflects a hardness, and the increasingly popular video games are anything but gentle. Has the world grown so vicious that it has infected our young people with such distrust and dislike for older generations, their music, their literature, their sensitivity, that they have become inured to a life in the hard lane?

Maybe we, as their parents, have let them down. Maybe ever since World War Two we've been too concerned with pursuing the "good life" and too removed from any true values. If that is the case then we have alienated our own children in the process. Have we yielded so completely to the desire for wealth that we have sacrificed our children to our selfish interests? I don't

know. It just seems like what we are witnessing is more than a single generational rebellion. It's already extended over several generations and shows no
signs of ever retrenching. I hope there will eventually be a point, as there has
been in the past, where the present generational course either reverses or mod-
ifies its direction into something more congenial.

When you're feeling crappy, it's easy to offload your misery onto something
or someone else. So, I guess that's what I'm doing. I could just have easily
vented my spleen on my own generation, or my parent's generation, or the
long history of man, or you name it. Seems nothing is ever perfect.

When I feel this bad I just let myself go and write a poem, about anything.
Today, for some reason, Winter appealed to me.

Snow-blown Winter's day.
Softly the grasses
Complain against the bitter wind,
While trees, protesting,
Toss their naked heads,
And lose the last
Of autumn's leaves.

Long years ago
I thrilled to such a wind,
And reached to feel the change,
And sense the prospect
Of hard times coming.

My eager youth
Presumed an elemental challenge,
That I longed to brave,
To prove my masculinity.

But now, the quiet child within me,
Remarks upon the wind's shrill voice,
And draws closer to the fire.

Day 94.

"…sustained and soothed…approach thy grave as one
who wraps the draperies of his couch about him and
lies down to pleasant dreams."

—William Cullen Bryant

❖   ❖   ❖

I think I may be feeling a little better although I feel so bad so continuously that it's hard to tell. I know I'm not eating well. I don't feel like eating when I'm sick and I don't know if that's good or bad. What is it? "Starve a fever, stuff a cold." Or, "starve a cold and stuff a fever." I never have gotten that right. So I just starve, figuring I'll get it half right anyway.

Last night my fever was pretty high, I think. I was kind of in and out of sleep and dreams. It got so I couldn't tell if I was asleep and dreaming or dreaming I was asleep. Now that's really screwed up. But, there I was not knowing which was which and in my dream or maybe not in my dream, I swung down from my tree like Tarzan in one of the old movies I remember as a kid, and I landed on my feet smoothly on the ground, and there in front of me was Jane. Not the Jane in the Tarzan movie but my wife, cast as Jane in my movie. And, I reached out and took her in my arms and swung up into the trees again. It never occurred to me at that time just how I could hold my wife in my arms and simultaneously clutch a vine and pull myself and her into the air in a giant swing upward. I think even in my dream I assumed at that point that it must be a dream.

That was the nice part, because when I got Jane into my palatial hideaway in the trees there was the friendly chimpanzee that was always in the movie with Tarzan and Jane. I think "Cheetah" was his name. And, there was Cheetah up in the rafters of my palace in the trees welcoming us home.

And, then the little bastard shit on me. Right on my head and I dropped Jane and she fell into the black space stretching interminably below.

I woke up covered with sweat. I was afraid to wipe my face for fear it would be covered with monkey dung. I don't know if I'll ever tell the story of that dream to my wonderful wife. She might divorce me for dropping her.

Day 95.

"…my white plume."

—Rostand

❦   ❦   ❦

People should smile more. Smiling lifts the wrinkles in one's face not to mention their spirits and those of everyone around them.

Not long ago, although after 96 days here in the tree it seems like forever, I was just going into a store when a very pretty, middle-aged woman was exiting. When we approached one another she smiled. Not just a grin or one of those quick, non-memorable, curving of the lips upward smiles, but a full mouth, almost laughing, flash of bright teeth, and a sparkle of sunshine from happy eyes. She said a genuine "Good Morning," as we passed.

It was such a pleasant shock that I just stood for a moment inside the door thinking what a delight it was to see her smile and what I took for her seeming joy at just being alive. At that moment I should have run outside, and thanked her for her lovely smile and for brightening my day.

Of course, I didn't. I've regretted that.

The time of Spring sings
Softly in my memory,
In years before
My reckoning of time,
When Winter's pall
Stopped short upon the dawn,

And the earth
Began to breathe again.

Day 96.

"I have seen the mermaids singing each to each,
I do not think that they will sing to me."

—T. S. Eliot

❧   ❧   ❧

There was an old man sitting on a bench one day in front of the hardware store I was about to enter. His face was so dramatic I couldn't help but stare at him, at least for a few seconds.

His hair was gray and shaggy and his full beard matched his hair but with slightly more gray in it. It all framed a face of wrinkles, large eyes, and a dominant reddish nose. His eyes were sad, full of acceptance and resignation, and spoke of deep and difficult struggles. His clothes were worn and disheveled without any distinction as to where sleeves or pants began or ended.

But his face, surrounded by all that shaggy mat of hair, was magnificent, still strong but tamed by life, at once startling but gentle, more than picturesque, it bespoke a chronicle of that man's life.

I captured that face with the camera I carry in my mind but I longed for a real camera and his permission so I could preserve the image of that old man's face and the vestiges of his life that it portrayed.

I thought of asking if he would wait for me to get my camera and if I could then take his picture. But I thought that might offend him. So, of course, I didn't. Now, I wish I had. When moments like that present themselves a person should follow their intuition and do whatever is necessary to make the moment live.

Day 97.

Deathly sick…can't write much today. Just got to hold on…four more days.

Remembering an old girl friend. She put me through hell and I was dumb enough to let her do it. I actually thought I was in love. In lust was more like it. Young men are so stupid when it comes to girls with pretty faces and big pontoons.

I don't think this girl ever had a serious thought in her life. She probably still hasn't. Anyway, I lucked out and woke up just in time to avoid a disastrous marriage.

This got me to thinking about people who will never in their entire lives examine themselves. I have spent many, many hours reviewing my own life, my egocentricity, my selfishness, my relationships, my cockiness, my arrogance, my bad moments, as well as some good ones. I must say that it takes a certain amount of determination and fortitude to admit to some of one's shortcomings. I haven't been all that I should have been but who the hell has. We just are who we are at a given time and that is really all we can be.

This old girl friend, and she really is old by now, will probably never understand why I ended our affair so abruptly. She will never take any responsibility for it. She will never question her actions and her contribution to the breakup. She will forever blame it all on me and I will forever be, in her memory, "The dirty rotten bastard."

Day 98.

"Who ever anywhere will read these written words?"

—James Joyce

❧   ❧   ❧

I'm struggling to stay awake; all I want to do is sleep. I don' t know why I just don't give it up and go down. I really want to. But I'm so close. I jst can't quit now. But it's hard to think and i know I'm making mistrakes but I'll let the speil checker catch them.

I think i'm halucinating a lot. It's really difficult for me to keep my head on straight. I keekp seeing birds flying over my head but i can't see over myu jhead, theres a tarpul…tarpalll…cover over it.

I con't write anymor e it's to hard.

Day 99.

❧   ❧   ❧

I'm better today…i don't feel worse…I slept for…I don't know…most of two, three days…I can't quit now…not with only two days to go…my fever and chills are still in full force…I'm headachy and somewhat nauseous…I sleep most of the time…I'm not getting better but…at least I'm lucid…I think.

…hasn't rained in several days and the sun has poked through the clouds…at intervals and let me revel in its warmth…I do so miss the little things that I had begun to ignore…that I just took for granted…my life in a tree has taught me a lot about myself and…things truly important in a man's life…like a wife…and companions…and safety from the elements…and food…and scotch…oh, yeah, scotch.

What I wouldn't give for a bottle of highlands…single malt…scotch right now—I used to drink a lot more than I do now…it was a great pleasure to me…as were cigarettes…but I don't imbibe much anymore—old age is a bitch—it not only forces you to deprive yourself of the fun things in life like sex—alcohol—tobacco—fiery—foods—all the good stuff—and you have to submit to…ignominious—ignominious procedures…where every orifice of your body is probed…and x-rayed…and photographed…examined eight ways to Sunday—and you pay exorbitant sums to a doctor to put you through that torture...then you thank him—Ha!...it's like thanking Edward Albee...for forcing you to sit through *Who's Afraid Of Virginia Woolfe?*—not that I don't like Edward Albee or Virginia Woolfe...I didn't know either of them so I suppose I might like them.

What am I driveling on about?...only a butthead wouldn't know when to put the pen down...or in my case...laptop...but what the hell...it's better than just sitting here getting sicker...at least it keeps my mind off how rotten I feel.

What really pisses me off...is that I've subjected myself to this...insanity for umteen days...and I'll make it to the end or die...up here—but what the hell for? what did I think I was doing?—I can't for the life of me...remember what got me up here...I think I just wanted to be alone for a while...if that was it I succeeded...I deserve the price I'm paying for it.

Did I write about *The Grand Inquisitor?*...I should have...and poetry...I meant to include some poetry in this journal—I like poetry...not necessarily my own but other folk's...poetry is high-minded stuff and philosophy and all sorts of semantic claptrap.

What? What did I just say? I don't dare go back and read what I've put in the laptop...I tried one day and none of it...absolutely none of it made any sense—did I have a friend named Charlie? That's bizarre...the whole thing's bizarre.

Did I ever mention that my two biggest regrets were...too young for WWII...and too old for the sexual revolution?...I should have...I was born at an awkward time—I didn't care much for the latter part of the 20th century...the fifties were great...things went downhill after that—I don't know what I'm talking about most of the time...another flaw in my character...but I don't let that keep me from spouting off every chance I get—I really wanted to write some poetry up here...but it's tough to write anything—I'm not thinking too straight...and my eyes water a lot...and don't focus too well...if it weren't for the little...bumps on the...index finger keys...I wouldn't know where to put my hands on the laptop...maybe that would be a blessing.

I'm just going to lie down a bit—reminds me of the poem by Robert W. Service...*Song of the Parson's Son*—I knew it a long time ago...where he's in his cabin in the Yukon alone...and he's dying...and he's kind of delirious...and if I can remember it—he says: "Old and weak, but no matter...there's hooch in the bottle still...I'll hitch up the dogs...tomorrow...and mush down the trail to Bill—it's so long dark...and I'm lonesome...I'll just lay down on the bed—(same thing I just said)—tomorrow I'll go...tomorrow...I guess I'll play on the bed...red—come Kit your pawny...pony—is saddled...I'm waiting dear...in the court—Minnie...you devil...I'll kill you...if you skip with that flossy sport—how much does it go to the pan, Bill?...play up...school...and play the game...our father which art in heaven...hallowed be thy name."—or something like that—then it ends with—"this was the song of the parson's son...as he lay in his bunk...alone...ere the fire went up...out—and the cold crept in...and his...blue lips...ceased to moan...the hunger maddened...mal-amutes...had torn him...flesh...from bone."—lovely scene...almost...as good as Virginia Woolfe—I hope...they're are no malatukes around—mala-nooks—mala—pukes—whatevr......

Day 106.

"Abruptness is an eloquence in parting..."

—Sir John Suckling

❧   ❧   ❧

According to my irate wife, they came to get me late on the hundredth day, and took me down in the basket. They said I was a *real* basket case. I guess I was because I've been here in the hospital now for five days while they've been pumping all kinds of things into me by one method or another. I didn't give a damn because my lights had gone out well before my rescuers arrived and only came back on a couple of days ago.

My high-roller friends were in earlier today, and each of them laid three hundred and thirty-three dollars and thirty-three cents on my prostrate body, and proceeded to laugh their heads off at the odds they had given me in my insane adventure. They all admitted it was worth the money to have the entertainment I had given them for three months.

I joined in the merrymaking to make my near-death experience appear easy and totally insignificant. I didn't want to show my emotion at seeing them again, I would have blubbered like a baby, and made an ass of myself. So I brought out all the macho I have left and told them the whole thing was a piece of cake and I'd do it again in a minute, if the stakes were high enough. I waited for the lightning strike but none came.

My poor devoted wife was really some kind of pissed off at me when she saw my almost lifeless form hoisted out of the basket. She's managed to berate me to the fullest extent possible given my weakened condition. But, she'll get over it in time.

My hundred days in the tree taught me a lot. I didn't expect it to be a learning experience. I only wanted to get away for a while. Well, I did that, and it turned out to be a hell of lot more than I bargained for. It showed me some things about myself that I had never realized before. Some things that are pretty homely when you stop to think about it.

First off I was intensely selfish in wanting to absent myself from everyone who cared about me. I didn't give a damn about them, I was only thinking of what I wanted. I know I'm a selfish bastard, I always have been. It's a flaw in my character.

I was also highly intolerant of my poor wife who wanted nothing more than for me to be safe and as well taken care of as she could from down below. I must show her how very much she means to me now that I have recovered my senses.

My selfishness led me to many other self-indulgences, such as writing without a care for anyone else, but then that has to be a forgivable sin since I don't think my writing will disturb many people, except those who read it.

But, up there, a strange thing happened. Suddenly I discovered how much those people and my connectedness with them really meant to me. Being alone, I mean totally alone, for all that time, made me realize my dependence on them, not just for the physical things they supplied me with while up in my tree, but their very presence, their being, their involvement in my life and my involvement in theirs. I found out that I was a part of a large family, including my friends, and moreover, that I sincerely wanted to be. I didn't want to be alone. I didn't want to be removed from the interaction and the vitality of them all. I wanted to participate, be with them, and enjoy them for who they are.

That was probably the most important thing I discovered but there were many other little things that I found were vitally meaningful to me. Things like continuity and routine in one's life; being able to recognize and appreciate the many joys present in our lives almost continually, like poetry, and humor, and music, and art, and other people, and conversation, and the beauty of nature in all the infinity of miracles around us; to revere the little things like a smile or a courtesy or just good manners in anyone and in yourself; to honor those that have gone before you for their lives and their stories; to prize time as our most precious possession, and make that time valuable by filling each minute with some recollection, or observation, or creativity, and not letting our absurd busyness keep us from grasping the significance of every moment of our lives; to indulge in a little absurdity ever now and then, if just to enjoy our freedom;

to love freely, for love exalts the lover, placing him above vanity, and pettiness, and meanness; to accept and even welcome change, looking upon it as something new and interesting; to admit everyone's reality and learn from them and their perspective so as to enable a better look at your own; to laugh at yourself for in all your sophistry you are undoubtedly laughable; to enjoy what you have, your life, your family, your friends, your place in the world, and in history.

All in all, it was a hell of an experience. I learned some things up there. Some important things. I'll try my best not to forget them.